The s ...... awled unconscious, and th ......

"Hey, ... o chick. You know, the—"

"Dead?"

"Naw. Out, though. Now how the hell . . . ?"

Perhaps ten seconds had elapsed since Bolan had left the girl's side. He could see four men closing in. He sighted into the hair trigger as one guy bent over to grab the girl. The blazing muzzle of the AutoMag executed a small arc and bellowed twice, the two reports coming together in a stuttering *ba-boom!* as the bending figure toppled and the other machinegunner spun off into dark oblivion with 240 grains of instant dispatch thundering up his nose.

Bolan's third round came out of a whirling dance and splattered through glass to find human flesh and bone, sending a shower of departing life forces spraying onto the man at the far side.

Round four overtook another man at the doorpost as he was spilling roundward in hasty retreat, helping him along, punching him down in a tumbling descent that rolled him over and laid him face-up on the cement.

One guy's eyes were open and aware. Bolan guided his good hand to the pressure point on the carotid artery as he quietly advised, "You can save something yet, Mario . . . If you make it, tell your bosses they're not going to work here. Not until they get past me."

The Executioner Series

the EXECUTIONER #21
FIREBASE SEATTLE
by Don Pendleton

PINNACLE BOOKS   •   NEW YORK CITY

This is a work of fiction. All the characters and events portrayed in this book are fictional and any resemblance to real people or events is purely coincidental.

THE EXECUTIONER: FIREBASE SEATTLE

Copyright © 1975 by Pinnacle Books, Inc.

An original Pinnacle Books edition, published for the first time anywhere.

ISBN: 0-523-00499-0

First printing, January 1975

Printed in the United States of America

PINNACLE BOOKS, INC.
275 Madison Avenue
New York, N.Y. 10016

For Big Larry Colman
who became immortalized in my household
during the writing of this book.
Bong-Bong.

dp

The god of the cannibals
will be a cannibal,
of the crusaders a crusader,
and of the merchants a merchant.
—Ralph Waldo Emerson
   (Conduct of Life)

Watch the man and you'll know his god.
I'm just helping all these boys to that
great Cosa Nostra in the sky.
Let it eat them.
—Mack Bolan, The Executioner
   (from his Journal)

PROLOGUE

Mack Bolan did not regard himself as a superman. He knew what he could and could not do; he knew his own strengths and weaknesses. And he had learned—in the school of life and death—that knowledge coupled with action and wedded to total commitment would elevate any ordinary man into the ranks of the extraordinary.

Superman, no; extraordinary weapon of war, yes—Mack Bolan was certainly that. He was a craftsman and his craft was warfare. It was a particular brand of warfare in which the warrior became either extraordinary or dead. Bolan remained alive. He had learned his craft well in the do-or-die theaters of Southeast Asia—and he had brought his diploma home to ply his trade in the untidy junglelands of America.

He did not think of himself as a crusader, nor even a patriot—though he was certainly both. He felt no grand exaltation in his self-appointed role as nemesis of the American underworld—though he was that, also—and he took no pride whatever in the knowledge that he himself was officially regarded by his own society as a part of that same underworld.

His name was at the top of the "hit list" of every Mafia family in the country. Freelancers and Saturday night warriors of every stripe swarmed his trail

1

with dreams of six-figure bounty dancing through their heads. Police establishments throughout the world kept dossiers on his known movements and activities, and he had dominated the FBI's top ten list since the beginning of his homefront war.

What sort of man, in the face of such incredible and overwhelming odds, keeps on keeping on?

In speaking of Bolan in his pregangbusting days, friends invariably describe him as a friendly, thoughtful, and kindly man. Aside from his programmed forays against the enemy in Southeast Asia, there exists no evidence whatever to suggest that he possessed a violent nature or even a vindictive streak. The record in Vietnam reveals again and again that he was respectful of the Vietnamese people, that he was responsive to the suffering of the children of that ravaged land, that he inspired lasting friendships and fierce loyalty from his comrades.

Military superiors respected and admired him.

The enemy—knowing him only by his code name, "the Executioner"—feared and despised him. Enemy commands, in fact, posted rewards for his capture or death.

Combat medics dubbed him "Sergeant Mercy," in recognition of his repeated services to Vietnamese victims of war.

The U.S. Army psychological profile of Sergeant Bolan sketched a portrait of a soldier who was self-commanding, nerveless, and responsive to "a sense of higher morality." Such attributes were considered mandatory for Penetration Team specialists. They had to be men of rare intelligence, self-sufficiency, and highly developed martial skills, with the ability not only to survive alone in enemy country but to wage effective warfare on an individual basis.

Sergeant Bolan was, indeed, an "executioner." This

2

was his specialty, his craft, his mission. He had been credited with ninety-five official "kills" of high-ranking enemy military and civilian officials.

Even in such an unpopular and "immoral" war, however, Mack Bolan had never alibied his "specialty" to anyone, newsmen and war historians included. He would and did tell them simply that he had not chosen this war; it had chosen him. He had not requested permission to kill the enemy; he had been trained and ordered to do so. He did not war *against* men but *for* ideals.

What sort of a man keeps on keeping on?

The sort, maybe, who can figuratively lay down his life, his identity, his whole reason for existence, in response to a high call to duty. Mack Bolan the man had died in Pittsfield at the gravesite of his mother, father, and kid sister. He had come home not a conquering hero but a grieving soldier on emergency leave—returning only to bury his own beloved dead.

Sam and Elsa Bolan, with daughter Cindy, had become victims of the American homefront. They had died as the victims of tyranny—the tyranny of "the invisible second government of America"—they had died in the brutalized land of *Mafia*.

And the "specialist" thereupon moved his war to a new front.

The Executioner was transported to the jungle-lands of America.

The new war was born. "I am going to smash them," declared one lone warrior who had learned to fight alone. "I am going to destroy the Mafia."

What sort of man? *Bolan's* sort.

3

1: SOFT TOUCH

Bolan wore combat black in modified paratrooper rig, a neck-slung auto pistol riding point as head weapon—snugly secured now for the jump—.44 AutoMag in backup at the right hip, belts crossing the chest beneath parachute harness to support a variety of hard-punch munitions. These were, however, "contingency" weapons. The mission was planned as a soft recon; there were also "soft-touch" weapons riding the military web. The hard stuff was for emergency punch-out purposes only.

Jack Grimaldi, an old friend from past campaigns, was at the controls of the Cessna skyjumper.

Conversation between the two had been minimal, geared entirely to the point of the problem at hand.

Now Grimaldi cleared his throat and shouted, "Coming around onto upwind. Altitude four thousand. Check that mark!"

Bolan leaned groundward through the jump hatch, then angled his blackened face into the cabin to shout back, "Correct five degrees starboard!"

The pilot made the necessary adjustment then reported, "Check! Course is now two-eight-five!"

They had already made the wind-marker drop, using night-glo nylon to calculate the wind-drift effect. The drop zone was firm. The time was minutes short of 2:00 A.M. It was a moonlit night with broken

5

clouds at eight thousand feet. A thin layer of stratus was forming at rooftop levels far below, like wispy ground fog. Another twenty minutes could see the entire area socked in.

Target was a small island in upper Puget Sound, just clear of the shipping lanes, with a total area of less than five hundred square yards. Smaller still was the desired landing area—a compound one hundred yards wide by two hundred long, a strong security area protected by high voltage fencing and roving patrols.

Intelligence estimates put a standing hard force of about thirty men on that island. They had not been there for long, nor had the security compound. Until very recently, the island had served as the residence of a Seattle-area millionaire recluse. Improvements had been limited to a smallish, modern mansion and a few guest cottages, a short pier and two-stall boat-house. Suddenly ownership had been transferred to an obscure Mafia front man, the security compound had gone up, hardmen had come in, and a mysterious construction crew from somewhere outside the area had worked an around-the-clock schedule to erect several new buildings—prefab jobs. The pier had been lengthened, and a storage building had been added to the boat area.

A new hardsite had been born almost overnight.

The only access was via boat or helicopter, and then only by the very highest-level invitation. According to Bolan's sources, such invitations issued not from anywhere in the state of Washington or adjacent areas, but from mob headquarters itself in New York—*la Commissione*.

All of which would strike the curiosity of a guy like Mack Bolan. Enough so that he would summon the services of Jack Grimaldi and take a crash course in precision skydiving.

But this was to be Bolan's first nighttime jump. And he was dropping into a hostile zone, guided only by his own unique combat sense and a few dim lights on a tiny plot of ground four thousand feet below.

And now the moment had arrived.

Grimaldi cupped his mouth with one hand and yelled, "Tally ho!"

Bolan's only response was a glinting of icy eyes— then he was launching himself through the hatch in a swan dive and hurtling through the black void of night.

He ate two thousand feet in a soaring free fall, limbs outspread and maneuvering into the desired drift path, the earlier exhilaration of practice jumps replaced now with grim concentration and do-or-die purpose as the dark waters of Puget Sound rose up to meet him.

The twinkling lights of the target zone were far downstream and there was nothing but water directly below when he pulled the cord and took the jolt that sent him swinging into a controlled descent on a straight downwind run toward paydirt. It was a small, precision-control chute of black nylon which under ordinary circumstances would lower him at a rate of descent of about twelve miles per hour. With the payload Bolan was carrying, the rate was probably more like fifteen to eighteen m.p.h.

He broke land at an altitude of about 500 feet, moving on downwind beyond the far end of the compound before circling upwind for the final drop —and this maneuver gave him an excellent bird's-eye view of the layout down there as he glided silently overhead.

7

The main house was crowded pretty close to the front fence—at a distance of perhaps 100 feet from the boat landing, well above sea level. Neatly manicured grounds spread across that upper level, with covered walkways leading to the guest cottages which were fanned out to the rear. About fifty yards of grass and shrubs separated the cottages from the new construction site—three long buildings set side by side and constructed of corrugated metal—like small warehouses. Another thirty yards or so of lawn and flower gardens stretched from that point to the back fence.

Bolan's angle of approach carried him directly along the shoreline to the side, circling back for touchdown just inside the rear fencing, and landing with a jarring thud that set feet and legs tingling.

Seconds later he'd succeeded in collapsing the chute, rolling it into a manageable bundle, and heaving it over the fence. It plunged on, billowing and popping with newly trapped wind as it scudded off into the night and toward the back side of the island. With any luck at all, it would carry on into the sound and drift clear.

Bolan moved silently in the opposite direction, blending with shadows wherever available and following tendrils of wispy ground fog—sizing, reading, pausing now and then to sift sounds from the night—but moving steadily toward the dim outside lights of the "warehouses."

Two men with choppers awaited him there, loitering in the shadows of the end building and peering nervously into the misty darkness toward the rear of the compound. As Bolan hove into audio range, one of them was quietly insisting, "I tell you, I heard something back there."

"So go check it out," replied the other with soft sarcasm.

"I guess it's just gulls," the first sentry decided, backing off.

"Naw, it's probably gangbusters. You better go check it out."

"Go to hell," the first guy replied, chuckling.

Bolan meanwhile was flanking them, coming up stealthily on their blind side, moving into "soft weapon" range. He was scouting, not blitzing, and wished to leave no evidence or even suspicion of his visit. The small medicated darts of the TranGun, a double-barreled compressed-air marvel of American technology, would give instant knockdown, a quick drunk, the torpor of twilight sleep for several hours, and nothing worse than a whiskey hangover in the aftermath.

The problem for Bolan, in this application, was to get in close enough without being seen, then pump them both before either became aware of the attack.

And he did so, *phutting* the little darts in just below the ear on each sentry in a quick one-two. They staggered backward simultaneously, hands going to the necks in reflex and staying there as both men sagged against the building and slid to the ground.

One of them was making drunken sounds with a thick tongue and stroking his burpgun as Bolan retrieved the darts; the guy saw Bolan, all right, but there was no flicker of perception in those clouded eyes. If he were to remember anything at all, it would be in the nature of a vague dream.

Bolan went on, found two other sentries patrolling the forward grounds as singles, and he soft-touched them also.

9

Next he invaded the house, discovered a nightman at solitary vigil in the kitchen with a sixpack of Hamm's and a transistor radio softly playing, and he beddy-byed this one just as softly.

A quick shakedown of the house revealed no other human presence. No clothing in closets or dresser drawers—no personal effects in the bathrooms other than sealed, unused toiletries—no evidence whatever of habitation by anyone.

Returning to the kitchen, Bolan found beer, cokes, and packaged sandwiches in the refrigerator—nothing else. A chef's pantry was well larded with canned and packaged foods; a large chest-type freezer was well stocked with steaks and chops—but it all had the appearance of something *waiting* to be used rather than in current use.

The guest cottages just had to be bunkhouses for the hard force. Bolan elected to leave them alone, proceeding instead to the three long buildings of corrugated steel.

Each was double locked.

He found keys among his early victims, and hit it lucky. But what he found in that first building staggered his mind.

Towering mounds of soft earth—rocks piled everywhere—heavy equipment of every type—open shafts descending into the earth.

The building was nothing but a cover for some fantastic kind of excavation project.

The center "building" held the key to understanding. It was clean in there—freshly so—and smelling of new paint. Bolan found the stairway and descended into stygian blackness, a small pencil-flash showing the way.

Twenty feet down, he found it.

A bunker.

10

Believe it or not—a damned bunker. And a very VIP one, at that. Lavishly outfitted, sleeping accommodations for eight, elaborate galley, comfortable game room with dart boards and card tables, large television console. Tunnels going off at various angles.

The whole thing was built into solid rock.

What kind of paranoid . . . ?

Bolan made quick sketches and got out of there. He returned the keys to the sentries and made a quiet withdrawal to the front gate where another key from another peaceful sentry passed him through the electrified fence and onto the boat landing.

He went all the way to the end of the pier, then sent a flare shell whizzing skyward. If the luck held, Grimaldi would begin a low-level run precisely sixty seconds later. He would drop a rubber boat fifty feet off shore. Bolan would be on hand to receive it, and he would drift to the next island downstream which just happened to feature a small landing strip.

But the warrior's mind was not dwelling at that moment upon the details of a routine withdrawal exercise. He was thinking instead of whispered words gleaned from electronic surveillance devices here and there about the country over the past several months.

The word "Seattle" had kept cropping up in tersely guarded and coded conversations . . . and also the word "firebase," in the same context of intrigue.

And now Bolan's mind was putting it together.

The mob was brewing something big in or around Seattle.

Was Langley Island what the whispers were all about?

He inflated a watertight flotation bag, secured his

11

weapons in there, and heaved it into the Sound, then dived in after it.

Sure. A firebase could mean many things to many people. A forward post for an artillery company. A sort of base camp for marauding bands of forward infantry, with artillery support.

Heavy, though. The word was heavy for everybody.

And it was heavy for Mack Bolan.

The mob had something big cooking, something *really* big. Big enough to code Langley Island as a *firebase* and to spend God knew how many millions of bucks putting it together. *Solid rock*—like a command bunker.

And, sure, that was it. Had to be.

The boys were going to make the big reach. They were getting ready to try for all the marbles. *Cosa di tutti Cosi*—the Thing of all the Things—they were putting it together, on Langley Island, of all places, believe it or not.

And why not? Seattle was a major seaport. Canada was just a few miles away, accessible by water. Major trade routes to Alaska swept right past the island itself. *Alaska!*

Some big things were shaping up for Alaska— *spectacular* things involving billions of dollars. Not to forget the Orient, and the many new trade routes opening to that section of the world.

Firebase Seattle?

Sure, why not—it explained many odd developments in the world of Mafia over the past few months. They were getting ready to rape the world. The Pacific Northwest was virgin territory, more or less. What better place to conceal clandestine operations? Who, but Bolan, would believe it? Who then, but Bolan, could stop them?

12

Firebase, indeed! Combat headquarters for the whole damn underworld infrastructure, that's what it was meant to be—the new multinational capital of the planet Earth.

Somehow, Mack Bolan *had* to stop them.

Somehow, dammit, he *meant* to stop them!

2: CRITIQUE

The big cool guy was waiting for him when Grimaldi put the Cessna down at the rendezvous point.

"How'd it go?" the pilot asked the blitz artist as he sent the little craft plunging into the take-off roll.

"Perfect," old ice-eyes replied, and that was all he said.

Grimaldi knew better than to press for conversation. Bolan would tell when and what Bolan wanted to tell. He was not the most conversational guy in the world. Especially at a time like this. Grimaldi had learned to respect the postcombative silences. Apparently the blitzer made a practice of mentally reviewing the events and immediate results of a hit while they were still sharply etched into the mind—a sort of one man combat critique or debriefing.

This time the big guy looked worried—or, at least, as worried as a guy like Bolan could get. Obviously the mission had produced more questions than answers.

Some kind of guy, this Bolan.

All ice and purpose, a battle machine, a deathmaker—and, yet, something much more than that. A superb tactician and strategist. Computer mind, body of an Olympic athlete. Nerveless, daring, *deadly*. Still, though, much more than all that. He was a *man*, dammit. A storybook kind of man. The things he did actually bothered the guy—all that death and hellfire he carried around with him—it weighed on the guy, burdened him. The self-appointed role did not sit easily upon the man. Yet he went on with it, campaign after grinding campaign, without hesitation, without alibis, without complaint. He had a job to do. He was doing it, the only way he knew how.

The two had been friends through a couple of those campaigns. It hadn't started that way, of course. Grimaldi was a Mafia pilot, a wheelman of the skies, a syndicate flyboy who was expected to enjoy his fat salary and keep his ears and mouth closed. He wasn't a "made man"—a full-fledged brother of the brothers—but on the payroll, just the same. So Grimaldi had known this guy Bolan from both sides of the street. He knew his threat—his effect—knew, even, that chilling, heart-shuddering sensation of looking at the guy over the wrong side of a gunsight.

There was something about Mack Bolan that caused even his enemies to admire him. Those who hated him most—and with the best reasons—still gave the big guy grudging admiration and genuine respect.

Grimaldi certainly had.

He'd flown the guy from Vegas to Puerto Rico, without realizing until the last leg of the journey that his passenger was Mack Bolan instead of the mob courier he was pretending to be. And, sure, Grimaldi had very naturally conspired with the forces at Glass Bay to ambush this most feared enemy of the new kingdom. It didn't work, of course. Bolan could have killed him then, but didn't—for some reason. Twice again at Puerto Rico Grimaldi had found himself

16

at the business end of Bolan's gun, and twice more the guy had let him live. The Caribbean chapter had closed with Grimaldi a committed ally of the Executioner—and for some damn excellent reasons.

Grimaldi loved the guy, like a brother.

There was no getting loose from the mob, of course —not while a guy was still breathing. It was a lifetime contract, from their point of view. So, sure, he still flew the wiseguys around and made a pretty good living doing it. And kept his eyes and ears open for a good buddy named Bolan. He also jumped quickly and willingly to work with the guy any time the invitation was sent.

Sure, he loved the big cold bastard. Bolan had held up a mirror to Jack Grimaldi's soul, reminding the former combat pilot what *manhood* was all about. Grimaldi liked the view. He liked his own image beside Bolan's.

And, getting down to basics, that was the only damn reason for any of it.

Grimaldi suspected that Bolan's own reasons were probably very similar. There were some things that a man—a *true man*—just had to do. Bolan was doing them. A man measured up to his own challenge. Bolan's challenge was just a bit more unique than the average.

And this time, yes, the blitzer had a worried look about the eyes.

They were headed for a small, private field just north of Seattle. Grimaldi broke the long silence of mutual critique to remark, "Pretty tough one, huh." He lit a cigarette and handed it over to his passenger.

The guy took a drag and handed it back. "Yeah," he replied as he slowly released the smoke.

"So what're they doing on the island?"

17

Instead of answering, Bolan responded with a question of his own. "How many flights have you made into here the past few months?"

"Here?" the pilot replied. "None. Two into Spokane, though."

"What's giving in Spokane?"

Grimaldi shrugged. "They never tell me. I only know that the fair was the cover. Expo '74, you know. My guys were supposed to be planning advisors. Something to do with the exhibits."

"From where?"

"One delegation was from Europe. I don't know where exactly. The other was from Tel Aviv."

Bolan blinked at that latter revelation. "Yeah?"

The pilot shrugged as he replied, "That's what the baggage checks on their luggage said. They flew into New York via Air Israel."

"Your reading?" Bolan asked quietly.

"VIPs from the international arms. Bosses, I'd say. Three in the first party, five in the last. Armed escort from New York, both times, full head parties. I flew them in the executive jet. That's reserved for nothing but the top."

"You flew them both in and out?"

"Yeah. Stayed a couple days, both times."

"So they could have come on to Seattle by car. Both parties."

"That's right," Gremaldi said, sighing.

"Anybody meet them?"

"Oh sure. Red carpet reception."

"Mob people?"

"None that I'd know," the pilot replied.

"I guess it figures, then," Bolan coldly commented.

"What figures?"

The big guy had produced his "warbook" and was jotting down something for future reference. In an offhanded tone, he told his pilot, "They're building a fort back there."

"On that island?"

"Yeah." Bolan was flipping the pages of the notebook, searching for something near the front. "You say they're using the Spokane fair as a cover?"

"That was the feeling I got. What kind of fort?"

"A little Gibraltar. Complete with tunnels and stonewall bunkers." Bolan had located the entry in his warbook. "Tel Aviv, eh. You ever hear of a ship called the S.S. *Piraeus Merchant?*"

"What is that—not Israeli?—no, I never heard it mentioned."

"It's Greek, and it's sitting down here in the Port of Seattle right now. Two weeks ago she picked up a cargo skid at Marseille, marked for storage-in-transit at Seattle. Has Expo '74 stickers all over it."

"What—the ship?"

"The skid. Supposed to be a crate of machinery. It's consigned to Nyeburg."

"Who?"

"Allan Nyeburg—the guy that bought Langley Island."

"Oh, *that* Nyeburg," Grimaldi replied, scowling. "Never heard of him either, thanks."

Bolan chuckled solemnly. "Don't feel bad. Neither has anyone else. But they will."

Grimaldi shivered slightly for poor Nyeburg, whoever the unfortunate soul might be.

Bolan sighed and closed the warbook, then glanced at his watch and took a look outside. "I guess there's time," he said.

Grimaldi was lining into the runway lights, on final approach, the field barely visible through the growing fog blanket below. He withheld comment until after the touch down. The fog was actually a bless-

19

ing. There was no tower here—just a base operator's maintenance hangar and a tie-down area for private craft. Bolan had left his "warwagon" concealed somewhere up beyond the end of the runway, where Grimaldi would drop him off.

He continued the landing roll to that point then swung clear and braked to a halt. "Time for what?" he asked the big grim man beside him.

"Maybe a hard punch to the belly, before daylight."

"Need me?" the pilot asked.

"Not for this one," Bolan replied. He was getting his gear together.

"Thought you were staying soft for a while."

"The soft drill is over, Jack," Bolan told him.

"I see." The guy who loved Mack Bolan like a brother tried and failed to smile. "Are you telling me to get lost now?"

"I'd like for you to stick around for a day or two if you can. Could get hairy, Jack. I could need you."

The grin worked this time. "You know where I'll be," Grimaldi said, quietly glowing.

Bolan gripped his hand, smiled as only a life-and-deather like Bolan can smile, and stepped out of the plane. A small bundle was left on his seat.

The pilot yelled, "Hey! You left something!"

"It's not mine," the big guy called back as he disappeared into the mists of the night.

Not his, bullshit. Ten grand, in hundred-dollar bills.

Grimaldi stuffed it inside his shirt and taxied on to the hangar. He wasn't working for Bolan's war chest bucks, dammit. That smile and that handshake was plenty payment enough. But Bolan would never have it that way. The guy liked to pay his tab. Nothing personal. No friendships, no debts, nothing asked and nothing accepted.

What a rotten way for a guy like Bolan to have to live!

Grimaldi would not argue with success, though. The guy *was* alive, and that was saying plenty right there. And Jack Grimaldi, the capi's flyboy, would gladly burn the whole ten grand for a ringside seat at Bolan's next blitz.

But, hell no—he would not argue with that guy's formula for success.

Grimaldi remembered Vegas—and the Caribbean —and Texas. He'd been there. Sure, he remembered. And he found himself feeling just a bit sorry for Seattle.

3: PERSONAL TOUCH

Bolan had scouted that wharf area several days earlier, shortly after the Greek ship had docked. He'd watched as they rigged the cargo booms and began the offloading, and he'd joined the stevedores down on the wharf as the stuff started coming ashore —working alongside them in Levi's and dungaree jacket. He'd also located the suspect shipment and put his mark on the crate as it moved along to the transit storage area in the warehouse. Later he'd split a hundred dollars between a couple of warehouse-men to "misplace" the crate for a few days—and he'd hung around long enough to watch where they put it.

He had not really known, at the moment, just why he should be especially interested in the shipment, or if it held any meaning whatever to the developments around Seattle. It was simply another of those isolated pieces of an international jigsaw puzzle which kept turning up in his intelligence notebook. Until then he had never heard of Allan Nyeburg or Langley Island. But he'd heard rumbles from several sources concerning "a lot of stuff" moving by way of Marseille, the "hot port" of Europe, and he'd been spot-checking shipping manifests from that area ever since the Texas campaign. So it could have been a stroke of luck—or the questing finger of fate—that

23

turned this shipment to Bolan's attention just as he was opening his probe into Seattle.

The resulting investigation of Nyeburg himself had nothing to do with luck or fate. It had been a simple job of softshoe scouting, asking questions in the right places, getting access to certain files and records—and putting the package together.

It was an impressive one. And it had led directly to Langley Island.

Nyeburg was among the newest of the new wave of front men lately being fielded by the syndicate, around the world. He was "clean," well-educated, fairly young, considered brilliant in various areas of international trade and finance. In Bolan's notebook, Nyeburg was now acting as some sort of advance man for the big push at Seattle.

Discovery of the intrigue on Langley Island had served to sharpen Bolan's curiosity about the crate of "machinery" from the S.S. *Piraeus Merchant*. So now he'd returned full circle to the beginning—and he intended to have a look at that shipment.

He came, this time, in blacksuit—with the .44 AutoMag in open display at his right hip, traveling light, the warwagon parked two blocks over and poised for a quick split.

The fog was in pretty good control of the wharf area, overlaying the blackness of the night like a damp woolen blanket and making dim haloes of the warehouse lights. The dark bulk of the *Piraeus* loomed mysterious and ghostly in the mist-shrouded dock, dim gangway lights twinkling like fireflies in the gloom.

Farther down, at the storage warehouse, things were happening. The big cargo doors were open, muffled light spilling out to mingle in shining shrouds with the moist atmosphere. A truck was parked down there, backed halfway into the warehouse. Forklifts were whining around, moving freight or something about the interior.

It was not an entirely unexpected development for Bolan, even though he had earlier ascertained that no night shifts worked this particular wharf. He had, in fact, called his warehousemen friends twelve hours earlier and instructed them to "find" the misplaced shipment and to notify the consignee.

Now the man in black was penetrating deeper for a close look at the situation, combat senses alert and flaring into that no man's land between dockside and warehouse, the AutoMag sprung and ready for instant use.

A dim human form materialized directly ahead, less than fifty yards from paydirt. Bolan froze, noisily cleared his throat, then coughed lightly and moved on more slowly.

A Bronx voice snarled, "Who's there?"

"It's me," Bolan replied, using the same Bronxese but with a less belligerent tone. "How's it going?"

"How would I know? Nobody tells me nothing." The guy was obviously a forward lookout. He was also ripe for picking. That voice revealed that its owner had been standing there quite a while—tense, uncomfortable, irritable.

And he was now moving cautiously toward Bolan, probably trying for a better view.

"Go down there and tell 'em I said to hurry it up," Bolan commanded gruffly. "Get some coffee while you're at it. You sound half asleep."

"Guess I am. Thanks. I'll tell 'em."

The guy turned and shuffled away.

Bolan immediately moved quietly along the backtrack. The lookout had accepted that "voice of authority" all too readily. Which meant, to Bolan, that others were waiting somewhere back there in the darkness of the waterfront. In a parked car, probably. Maybe a crew leader and a couple of guns. Bolan could not let that remain at his back.

He withdrew the way he'd come, then circled quickly and quietly for the only different angle of approach—and he found them there, just up the street from the *Piraeus* dock, two men in a big car with a lonely vigil.

The vehicle had been parked there a while, as evidenced by the even collection of fog droplets. The wipers had been operated as the car sat, to keep the forward vision unimpaired—and there was evidence of a continuing fogging problem inside, as well. The two front windows were cracked open about three inches from the top, the glass surfaces covered with the fine droplets of accumulated moisture without and condensation within.

Both men were smoking. As Bolan drew nearer, he heard the radio playing soft music. The guys were relaxed, slouched in the seats, bored. He moved softly to their rear, opened a back door, and slid onto the seat behind them.

The guy at the wheel snapped his head in a quick swivel rearward, mouth open, eyes flaring.

Bolan cautioned, "Uh-uh" and gave him a good look at the big silver pistol.

The other guy just sat there, eyes glued to the rearview mirror, frozen. But he found his voice first. "What the hell is this?" he blustered.

"Doomsday, maybe," Bolan informed him. He tossed a marksman's medal forward. It hit the windshield and fell to the padding atop the dash. "Pick it up," he commanded chillingly.

The wheelman did so, moving slowly and care-

26

fully, turning it over and over between thumb and fingers, otherwise immobilized, speechless.

The guy beside him growled, "What is it?"

"A bull's-eye cross," the wheelman declared in a loud stage whisper.

"Aw, Jesus," the other guy said, the voice dismal and demoralized. "That's not Mack Bolan back there."

"It is," the Executioner assured him. "Who're you?"

The guy had decided to try the chummy approach. "I'm Danny Trinity. You never heard of me, I guess. I heard plenty about you, guy. This big dummy at my left hand here is Ontario Charlie Flora, my wheeler."

That took care of the introductions, and Danny Trinity ran out of wind right there. Bolan was interested in further conversation, however.

"You boys might live a while if you play it right."

They understood what that meant, of course. Few living "made men" could boast of having once chatted with the Executioner. So if he was talking instead of blasting, there was double the usual hope right there.

"We got no beef with you, guy," Danny Trinity reported, apparently clinging to hope through a very obvious bravado.

"Keep it that way, then," Bolan advised. "Who're you with?"

The two hardmen locked eyes for a moment.

Bolan warned, "Keep it straight. You're talking to a guy who knows when you're not."

Ontario Charlie took a gulping half-breath and plunged on toward hope. "We're by way of Augie Marinello."

Okay, that hung straight enough. Marinello, though maimed by a clash with Bolan during the

27

Jersey war, still clung to life and to his position as most powerful New York boss.

Coldly, Bolan asked, "How is Augie?"

"What's left of 'im, okay," Danny Trinity sniffed. "You didn't leave 'im much, guy."

"I could leave you less," Bolan reminded the torpedo. "Where do you rank?"

"Nowhere," the *mafioso* replied, a bit less huffily. "I work a crew under Tony Vale."

"Enforcing," the ice man said.

"Yeah, sure. Look—you want my life history? I was born in—"

Bolan growled, "Save it. You're a long way from your territory, Danny."

The guy shrugged and angled a desperate toss of the eyes to his partner. "We're on vacation," he muttered.

Bolan lightly gouged the back of his head with the muzzle of Big Thunder. "This piece is a hand howitzer," he told the guy coldly. "It spits 240 grains of hollow-nose disintegrators with a muzzle energy of more than a thousand foot-pounds. The trigger moves very eagerly to a two-pound pull. All I have to do is sigh a bit too hard and your skull will fall in like a rotten egg. And every time you say something silly, Danny, it makes me sigh with regret."

"Okay, okay," the torpedo said, voice ragged and choking with defeat. "It *is* a sort of vacation. We're on loan. We been out here three weeks now, and this is our first job."

"How many boys with you?"

"I brought a crew of six, plus myself. That includes Charlie boy, here."

"What's the job?"

"*This* one? Hell, a milk run. We thought. The

locals are picking up some stuff at a warehouse down here. We're riding shotgun, that's all."

"Where are you shotgunning it to?"

"To another warehouse."

"Another warehouse *where?*"

"Up near Everett. Know where that is? Just up the coast."

Sure, Bolan knew where. Langley Island lay in that area.

"Let's have your hardware," he told them. "I don't want to see more than two fingers at a time. You first, Danny. Ease it out and pass it back."

There were no arguments in that regard. The hardmen seemed almost happy about it, as though their salvation was thereby assured. Bolan did not have a reputation for "killing cold." They carefully divested themselves of offending weapons and passed them back, one at a time. Bolan threw them to the street and told the wheelman, "Okay, Charlie, let's move."

The guy started the engine before inquiring, "Where to?"

"Onto the wharf, down to the warehouse."

The two men up front exchanged glances, then Ontario Charlie shrugged and set the car into motion. "Lights on or off?" he asked.

"Off, till I say different. And keep it slow."

"Wait a minute," Danny Trinity protested. "You know how many people there are waiting for you down there? There's my four boys plus four locals. None of 'em are what I'd call peaceful citizens. They all get their kicks from the big boom sound and they don't fuck around with formalities when that time comes around. You can't just—"

Bolan interrupted the tirade with, "You worried about my hide, Danny?"

29

"Hell no, I'm worried about mine. I don't wanta be in no crossfire between you people."

"Then you play it just like I tell you," Bolan suggested. "Down the wharf, Charlie, slow and easy. Move it."

The wheelman moved it. They rolled onto the wharf and began a slow progression toward those muffled lights at the far end. Danny Trinity slumped into the seat, staring tensely and stonily forward through the enshrouding mists. "Some guys are suckers for suicide," he growled, fear resurfacing and rippling the voice. "I thought higher of you, Bolan."

So did Bolan. He had no belly whatever for suicide. But he told his captives, "Everyone dies sometime, boys. I guess it's going to be up to you whether this time is our time. Play it cool and maybe it's just *their* time. Get dumb for just a heartbeat and I guess it's time for all us crazy bastards."

"I'm not a crazy bastard," the wheelman said with a shiver.

"Show me," Bolan suggested. "You too, Danny. Show me how sane you can be."

But Bolan was not betting a nickel on the sanity of those two. He was betting entirely on himself.

4: DEATH TOUCH

The AutoMag was a most impressive weapon. Developed by a West Coast gunsmith in the late sixties after years of frustrating trial and error, the autoloading .44 magnum was a triumph of weapon technology. The huge handgun measured eleven and a half inches from tip to tip, weighed three and a half pounds unloaded, and was constructed mostly of stainless steel. It was strictly a man's weapon—preferably a big man. It took a rather large hand and a well-developed grip to comfortably handle the piece. Designed primarily as a hunter's handgun, the big silver pistol would do most anything that a big-game rifle would do, except in extremely long-range situations.

The heavy loads in .44 magnum hollow-nose had hi-shock and instant knockdown capability at more than a hundred yards—which is the length of a football field. Bolan made his own ammo of cutdown .308 brass, using a powder charge of twenty grains behind a bullet of 240 grains, which produced a muzzle velocity of about 1400 fps. With such loads, the performance of the slickly-engineered weapon was truly outstanding and remarkably uniform. At twenty-five yards in combat stance, Bolan could rip a one-inch bull out of a target in rapid-fire. At a hundred yards, using a two-hand stance and firing deliberately, he could consistently group a full clip of the big bullets into an area the size of a man's head.

And that was some shooting.

Bolan had, of course, been a remarkable marksman since early in his army career. During those earlier years, however, his chief interest lay in the weapons themselves—the technical end. He was an armorer, with an almost instinctive understanding of weaponry from the very beginning. Any weapon is of course only as good as its performance, and Bolan's growing interest in that consideration led him inevitably onto the firing ranges and then into competitive matches where his phenomenal eye and cool self-possession won him championships in various weapons categories.

For more than a year he had toured the country for the recruiting service, staging marksmanship demonstrations and—toward the end of that period —trick-shot shows, using rifles and handguns.

The traditional combat stance for shooting competitions is a sort of head-on crouch, knees slightly bent, weapon extended straight out from the chest in one hand, with emphasis on rapidity of fire and reload. Bolan had usually performed these demonstrations with a standard army version of the .45 Colt autoloader, and his speed was dazzling—ejecting spent clips and reloading in less than one second. As a variation of this routine, the youthful Bolan developed some interesting choreography for his audiences, changing stance with lightning speed— from combat to prone and rolling prone—while reloading and continuing to fire with incredible accuracy. He performed similar routines using a thirty caliber carbine and a light auto.

Then came Vietnam, and Sergeant Bolan's expertise was diverted into more serious applications of soldiering.

Now here he was on the Seattle waterfront, the formidable .44 at the ready—trick-shot time again with all his expertise invested in the outcome.

It was not a situation he would normally choose for himself. He much preferred to be in full command of a battle situation, from the planning stages outward. If anything at all developed here, it would be more in the nature of a firefight—a play-it-by-ear sudden confrontation with all the odds riding on the side that played it the quickest and the trickiest.

There were, of course, one or two items which he could partially control. And he did have the advantage of surprise to partially offset the superiority of numbers on the other side.

The jokers in the deck were, of course, Flora and Trinity—his nervous companions of the moment. There was no way of knowing what they would do once he cut them loose on their own. Bolan could only try to influence that open question.

"Okay, stop right here," he commanded the wheelman. They had reached the point where Bolan had earlier encountered the lookout. The guy was nowhere in sight now.

Ontario Charlie brought the big car to a smooth halt.

"Turn on your parking lights!"

The wheelman did so.

Trinity was glaring tensely ahead. "They're still loading down there," he observed glumly.

"How many boys you say?"

"Eight, dammit. Eight damned mean boys. This is crazy."

"Only as crazy as you make it," Bolan reminded. "I'm getting out here, but I'll be no more than ten

33

paces to the rear. At that range, Danny, I can shoot the eyes off a fly. You boys cruise right on down there, same speed we've been going. First bad move you make, I'll punch you. Soon as you start moving again, bring the headlamps up—high beam. Keep them there. Stop at the truck and just sit tight."

"Sit tight till when?" Flora croaked.

"Until the shooting starts. Then I suggest you dig a hole quick."

Danny Trinity laughed nervously. "It's still crazy. You can't take on eight mean boys alone."

"Watch me," Bolan told him, and stepped out onto the wharf. "Move it!" he commanded, and closed the door.

The limousine crept forward. The lights came up and choked on the heavy atmosphere, reflecting back to create a weird halo of light to the front.

Bolan fell to the rear and moved along the wall of the warehouse.

Halfway to target, two guys ran out onto the wharf beside the parked truck. The Mafia vehicle surged forward suddenly, horn blaring, picking up speed quickly in a heavy-footed acceleration.

Some guys just never knew when they were well off.

Bolan smiled grimly and punched them as he'd promised, four big rolling booms in rapid-fire sealing the fate of that plunging vehicle as the AutoMag leapt in full-throated response to the situation as an extension of the man himself. The rounds crashed in at shoulder level through the rear window in a deliberate search pattern.

They evidently found something. The limousine immediately heeled and tacked sharply to starboard, hit the warehouse, and went into a roll. Bolan sent three blind rounds thudding into the door on the

34

passenger side as the vehicle went over. He ejected the spent clip and fed in a reload as he moved around the wreckage and into direct confrontation with the two hardmen on the wharf. They were already unloading on him, although without effect—their fire wildly adding further havoc to the shuddering vehicle. Even at ten yards, the guys were no more than indistinct shapes in the misty light spilling from the interior—crouching and backing into the warehouse an arm's length apart.

The AutoMag roared twice again with blazing rapidity, the double fire track touching both targets simultaneously and punching them over onto their backs in a dual slide to doomsday.

So okay. Two down and six to go—if Danny Trinity hadn't been padding the headcount.

Bolan advanced to the open door of the warehouse and moved inside, presenting himself and inviting fire. None came.

A large cargo skid sat on the cement floor directly behind the parked truck. The big marine crate had been ripped open; the top and one end lay on the floor. Smaller crates were inside; others were stacked neatly on the bed of the truck. A guy in work clothes sat behind the controls of an idling forklift, his hands elevated, eyes scared. The lift was raised and bore a crate identical to those already loaded.

"Where are they?" Bolan growled.

The guy's head moved almost imperceptibly toward a glassed-in cubicle across the way.

"How many?"

"Two," the guy whispered loudly.

"You're betting your life on that number, you know."

"Means nothing to me," the guy said quickly. "They gave me a hundred bucks to cart this load. I

35

don't even know 'em. There's two left. And they got a woman hostage. I saw 'em duck into the office when the firing started."

It could be true. Bolan had suspected that Danny Trinity might be doubling his numbers. He told the guy, "Drive that forklift on out of here. Around the corner and up the wharf and don't stop until you clear the area."

The guy said, "Sure, sure"—relief flooding the voice. He ejected his load in mid-air. The crate struck the side of the truck, split, and spilled its contents onto the floor.

Some contents.

Automatic weapons, fully assembled, critical parts bandaged with grease paper.

The man on the forklift gawked in genuine surprise.

"Ball it!" Bolan commanded sharply.

The guy wheeled his vehicle clear of the debris on the floor and as he rolled past the man in black he shouted, "Watch it mate! They're real loonies!"

Bolan always watched it. As for the female hostage—he was not inconsiderate of an innocent life, but he had also learned the only way to deal with such a situation, where guys like these were involved.

He made a fast run across the open area, emptying his clip high into the office enclosure and instantly reloading as he made the move. Glass shattered and rained loudly onto the cement, producing a cacophony to the thunder roll of the big weapon. A woman's shrill screaming joined the tumult, only to be quickly shut off. A bulky figure rose up from the foreground of office furniture as the reports of a heavy-framed pistol joined the sounds of the moment. The guy was pretty good; it was only Bolan's agility in a firefight that rendered the counterattack

36

impotent. He checked his run, whirled, and reversed before the return fire could track onto him—and sent three closely spaced disintegrators whizzing into that standing target. The gun spun away with a scream, overturning furniture and office machines in the heavy fall.

Another voice in there yelled, "Hey, hold it, man!" It was a young voice, barely mature. "I got a lady in here with me! You back off quick or I splatter her brains all over the joint!"

"Counter-offer," Bolan called back. "You come out alone, hands clean. I'll let you keep walking all the way to the dock, brains and all."

"Yeah, and how many cops are waiting out there?" the youngster screamed.

"Cops, what cops? This is Mack Bolan. You've got about two heartbeats left to decide, soldier. Move it damn quick, and I'd better hear a splash at the end of the walk."

A momentary silence, then, "Hey, is that straight? That's you, Bolan? The big bad shit?"

"It is. Quick now. Move it!"

For all his reputation as a grim reaper, Mack Bolan was also known as a man of his word. His "releases" and "white flags" had become legend in the soldierly ranks of the enemy.

"You want me to jump in the fuckin' water?"

"That's what I want, soldier. Throw out your weapon and come running."

In a quick decision, the young hardman did so immediately. A snubbed .38 whizzed through the shattered window and skittered across the cement floor, followed quickly by the charging youth. Eyes tracked briefly onto the black-clad figure then bounced away with discomfort plainly reflected there as he loped past. He went on without a backward glance, slowing somewhat at the doorway. Then the figure disappeared into the mists and Bolan heard the muffled, tell-tale splash at the end of the run.

A blonde young woman staggered into view from the shattered office. Very pretty, despite the disheveled and terrorized appearance. She shrank back at first sight of Bolan, then changed her mind as he smiled and extended an arm for her. Gladly she fell into the protection of that half-embrace and allowed him to lead her toward the wharf.

"I'm—I'm . . ."

"Save it," Bolan quietly suggested. "The important thing now is to get out of here. The game may not be over yet."

It was practically a prophecy. They stepped onto the wharf and into the shadow of a gun held by Danny Trinity.

The crew chief was bleeding from the head and his right arm hung uselessly at his side, but a big Colt .45 was at full extension in the left hand and already blasting into the five-paces confrontation.

Bolan spilled the girl behind him and fired once from the hip. The big bullet chugged into Trinity's chest and sent the guy staggering backward. The second pop was pure combat reflex on Bolan's part, and it caught Danny Trinity in the soft underside of the tilted chin as he was going down, reaming on through and exploding out of the top of the skull in a gory exit.

It was the final straw for the girl. She passed out with a sick little moan.

Bolan hefted her to his shoulder, stepped over the very messy remains of Danny Trinity, and went on up the wharf.

And, yeah, the quiet drill was definitely over.

Everybody in this part of the world, including cops and capos, would know now that the Executioner had come to town.

And there were still too many loose ends remaining from the soft probes.

Aside from melodramatic considerations, what was the *true* significance of the new super hardsite on Langley Island?

Why was the American syndicate importing crateloads of illicit munitions?

Why were international arms of the mob sending high-ranking delegations into the Pacific Northwest?

Bolan did not have many intellectual answers to the specific questions—but an old familiar gut feeling was telling him that hell was brewing in this quiet corner of the U.S.

Of course, now that his presence was known here —or would be, shortly—things would begin blowing into place with a hellish acceleration. He'd know the answers soon—or he'd be dead. And therein lay the ultimate problem for Mack Bolan. He'd remained alive thus far by making a practice of remaining on top of a problem—not by staggering around behind it, in the dark and wondering what the hell was coming off. He'd have to get on top of this one quick, if he meant to survive Seattle.

So here he was carting away an unconscious girl— doubling his liabilities. Who was she? Why was she here? Was she simply an innocent bystander—and, if so, what possible reason could she have for standing by in such an unlikely spot at such a time of night? She was young, probably no more than twenty-one or so. Stylishly dressed, softly feminine— hardly the kind you'd find wandering the waterfronts in the dark of night.

Bolan would develop those answers, of course.

It was part of the reason he was carting her off—but only part. There were other considerations. He could not simply walk off and leave her lying there unconscious—not even assuming that the cops would be shortly making the scene. No matter how innocent she might be, the girl had definitely become entangled in a game of underworld intrigue. She could have seen things and heard things, the knowledge of which would disqualify her for continued life. At least two men had walked away from that firefight— alive and well and able to tell tales. Both knew of the girl.

No, he could not simply walk off and leave her there.

Later, he was to find several reasons to be damned happy he hadn't—as well as a couple of reasons to wish that he had.

For the moment, though, she was simply an unavoidable part of Bolan's world. A *living* part. And there were all too damned few of those.

5: DEATH TRAP

He rounded the corner and moved quickly along the street in a cautious withdrawal toward the war-wagon—a very special vehicle he'd acquired in New Orleans an eternity or so ago. The unconscious girl was draped over his left shoulder—not much of a burden at a hundred pounds or so but a bit slippery. It was the dress that was causing the problem, a silky little chemise sort of thing that seemed to have no reference whatever to the body beneath it—a rather delectable body even under such strained circumstances.

It was that high-rise bottom, Bolan realized, that was the center of the problem. His carrying forearm was locked in just below the swelling buttocks as the most practical point of purchase—and the elusive dress, which barely covered the point, anyway, simply was not playing ball with the situation.

Fifty paces off the wharf he elected to sacrifice a bit of female modesty in the interests of the practical realities of the matter, pausing to readjust the load and get a better handle on it, moving the slippery material up and over the problem area and placing a hand where it did the most good.

No sooner had that problem been righted than another presented itself. A twin beam of automobile foglights was moving along the street toward him, close to the curb and cruising slowly with a spotlight probing the sidewalk along Bolan's side of the street.

Cops, was Bolan's first reading—primarily because he had been wondering about the apparent lack of response to the gunfire on the wharf.

He quickly slid the girl down into a frontal embrace, positioned flopping arms about his neck, and held her there with her back against the wall of a building.

It was not much of a play, and he knew it, but it seemed the only thing available at the moment. The fog was not all that thick up here off the water, either; if it was cops, the thing could be touch and go. Mack Bolan did not gunfight with the law.

The spot of light had not touched them by the time the vehicle drew directly abreast, and Bolan was breathing easier as it moved on past into the mists. But there was something ominous about that car; from what Bolan could see, it did not have the appearance of an official police vehicle.

As if to substantiate that gut feeling, it halted one car length beyond Bolan's position, a door opened and a cautious voice with a most decided East Coast inflection quietly commanded, "Run the spot back along that wall."

Another door opened and Bolan heard heavy feet hit the pavement.

The spotlight danced rearward, momentarily catching and illuminating two figures on the sidewalk beside the vehicle.

And, no, it was not cops.

It was a hard force, and the two guys on the sidewalk were carrying Thompson subs without stocks— very ornery weapons, from any point of view.

Suckered!

He should have scouted the area better before committing himself to a fight on this turf!

Bolan did not—nor could he afford to—make many mistakes. In a game like his, every number was vitally important. But, yeah, he'd goofed on this one —miscalculated the enemy.

What hurt the most, in that realization, was the knowledge that this maneuver was a simple SOP for the mob. They frequently worked this way, in a "layered" operation. They'd used a front line force, "goats" for the actual work at the warehouse. Then a set crew just up off the scene, for direct support— Flora and Trinity. Finally a "saver" force cruising the backdrops, playing the rear—like a football defense with linebackers and safety backs playing a zone defense.

These dudes with the choppers were the saver force.

They'd heard the gunfire—and cruised, wondering, waiting, looking for a way to save the play in case it'd gone sour.

And these boys would be the cream of the defense.

All this flashed through Bolan's peaking combat consciousness as he lowered the girl onto her back and moved catlike to the street in a single bound. He came lightly to rest on the balls of his feet, poised and ready to strike with Big Thunder up and ready.

Trick shot time again, sure, and with no room whatever for anything less than absolute precision targeting. Each round would have to unerringly find a "death spot"—leaving not even a dying twitch to the trigger fingers. A defenseless girl lay sprawled unconscious in the shadow of those guns.

And now the spotlight had found the girl, revealing also bulky human shapes at the fringe of illumination—one slightly bent forward over the unconscious figure, the other stationed in firing readiness, head swiveled uprange, tense and alert.

Then a surprised discovery: "Hey, Mario! It's that broad!"

From the car: "What broad?"

"That Webb chick! You know, the——"

"Dead?"

"Naw. Out, though. Now how the hell . . . ?"

"So it *wasn't* cops! Get 'er in here and let's go!"

Perhaps ten seconds had elapsed since Bolan left the girl's side. He sighed into the hair trigger as the guy bent over to grab her, the big slug hurtling forth under tremendous energy to rip into the ear and topple its victim in a grotesque headfirst sprawl. The blazing muzzle of the AutoMag executed a small arc and bellowed again, the two reports coming together as a stuttering *ba-boom!* as the other machine gunner spun off into dark oblivion with 240 grains of instant dispatch thundering up his nose.

The third round came out of a whirling dance that put the attacker in the center of the street directly opposite the idling vehicle, and this one splattered through glass to find human flesh and bone, sending a shower of departing life forces spraying onto the man at the far side—one "Mario" who was then reflexing into probably the final "save" of a misspent career.

Round four overtook him at the doorpost as he was spilling groundward in hasty retreat, helping him along, punching him down in a tumbling descent that rolled him over and laid him face up on the cement.

The wheelman had lost the top of his head to round three.

End of saver force, and nothing saved.

Almost.

"Mario" was groaning and jerking around over there.

Bolan took the direct route—sliding over the roof of the car and coming down at the guy's feet. He kicked a fallen pistol out of reach and knelt beside him.

Round four had removed a chunk of shoulder then gone on to whittle at the neck near the base of the ear. Blood was spurting from the neck wound. More was soaking the fancy silk suit through the shattered shoulder. The guy's eyes were open and aware of his situation. Bolan guided the good hand to the pressure point on the carotid artery as he quietly advised, "Keep a pressure there. You may save something yet."

The guy's eyes thanked him, even while damning him.

"Mario who?" Bolan inquired.

The torpedo tried to say something but the machinery would not work.

Bolan showed him a bull's-eye cross then dropped it to his chest. "If you make it, Mario, tell your bosses they're not going to work it here. Not until they get past me."

He left the guy lying there in his blood and went to the girl, who was lying in someone else's blood. Lucky for her, she was still unconscious—it was quite a mess she was soaking up.

The distant wail of police sirens was now in the air. The girl was growing rapidly as a direct liability. She was going to slow him, perhaps fatally, but still he could not leave her there like that.

Bolan plucked her from the gore and returned her to his shoulder, examining her quickly with his hands to make sure that the blood glistening on her backsides was not her own. Then he quickly crossed the

45

street and took off on a trot for his waiting vehicle.

From the sounds of those sirens, the whole area was becoming a death trap. He'd already overplayed his numbers—and he was very quickly, now, running out of them.

Bolan did not duel with cops. But that was a one-sided affair. The cops sure as hell would not hesitate to open fire on this most-wanted man in the country. For those brothers in blue, Mack Bolan was the object of a nationwide "mad dog alert." Every cop in the country was under orders to shoot on sight—and to kill. Bolan was well aware of that.

So okay, that was their job. More than that, it was an obligation to their badge. Bolan understood that. He'd never asked for or expected a license to kill. But he also understood his own obligation.

Mack Bolan the man had died back there in Pittsfield at the gravesite of Sam and Elsa and Cindy. What was left was the Executioner, the human war machine, the hellfire guy who remained alive only to kill—and who killed only to remain alive so that he could go on killing.

That was the obligation. Remain alive. Carry the war to the enemy, at every opportunity, until the enemy remained no more. It was a war of attrition, with all the odds riding on the other side.

But there was another obligation, and this one was to the soul. That soul must remain human, and it must remain worthy if the battle were to have any meaning other than a silly stride through hell.

Call it square or old-fashioned or just plain ridiculous—Bolan couldn't care less what anyone called it—he called it basic reality, and he saw this war of his as a reenactment of the eternal struggle between good and evil.

Sometimes "good" had to carry a big stick and

even masquerade as "evil"—to be the equal to evil, without becoming an equivalent of it.

So, no—Mack Bolan did not make war on cops. They were soldiers of the same side—the "good" side, even if a few of them may personally be undeserving of the badge they wore.

And, right now, those soldiers of the same side were screaming along a disturbing pattern of containment that seemed to be bracketing the entire waterfront area.

Very possibly a death trap, sure—for a guy who refused to become the equivalent of evil.

6: SOFT TRAP

The warwagon was a twenty-seven foot GMC motor home away from home for the super-sportsman, a sleek front wheel drive vehicle with a special Toronado power plant and air-suspension tandem rear wheels. Bolan had picked it up in New Orleans and turned a couple of space age electronics genuises loose on her with an unlimited budget—then Bolan had added a few touches of his own. The result was what the moonlighting NASA scientist described as a "terran module"—a self-contained, fully instrumented "earth scout" ship.

Bolan called it a warwagon, and that it was. Not only could she scout, she could also fight—as had been ably demonstrated in New Orleans. But she was also war room, munitions lab, armory, and home for the warrior—a rolling base camp. Or a firebase.

He carried the girl to the rear and slid her onto a bunk, then covered her with a light blanket and returned amidships to the war room where he activated the police monitors and remoted them to the front panel. Next he skinned out of the combat suit and concealed it, replacing that attire with Levi's and sweatshirt and bright orange hunter's jacket. Heavy-framed yellow night glasses and a soiled hunting cap completed the transformation. Then he checked the girl and went forward to fire up, wondering idly about the longterm unconsciousness but more concerned about the grim exigencies of the moment.

The police frequencies were strangely quiet, as was the night itself; there were no more sounds of sirens. Which, from Bolan's understanding, meant not a damn thing.

He sent the impressive vehicle in forward motion, moving slowly in concession to the atmospherics out there as well as in the interests of properiety for the sake of any watchful eyes.

Sure enough, he made contact at the first crossing. A police car with beacon flashing had the intersection partially blocked. Two young cops with hands resting on gun butts were deployed to either side.

Bolan edged on to the bumper of the cruiser, then opened his window and beat the cops to the draw.

"Thank God!" he called out with a pretty good try at emotional relief. "Help me, I need help!"

One of the cops took a wary step closer and asked, "What's the problem, sir?"

These guys were in riot tog—helmets and all.

"This damn fog! I'm lost, and I have an emergency. I hit a curb back there and knocked my wife off her feet. She bashed her head. Lead me to a hospital, will you!"

The cop stepped back, mouth settling into grim lines, but the voice was regretful as he replied, "Sorry sir, we have an emergency, too. Take a right at the next corner and keep going till you hit the freeway. You'll find hospital markers there."

Bolan yelled, "Thanks!" and wheeled on through the blockade. He smiled moments later as the speaker above his head crackled with an exchange on a secondary police channel.

"Four Alpha Three, what's your situation?"

"On station, skipper. Nothing showing. Except a

lost motorist in a camper, looking for a hospital—wife injured. Clean."

"It's plenty bloody down here. Stay alert."

"Aye, sir."

Bolan mentally tipped a hat to the men in blue. To respond so quickly with such organization in the doggy hours of morning—Bolan knew what it required. Contingency plays, crack discipline, an alert force—and it was certainly no reflection on their abilities that Bolan had managed to slip through. This was a simple response to a gunfight report, evidently. These people didn't know, yet, who they were looking for.

Or, at least, they hadn't.

Now they did.

"All units, this is Reaction Control. The subject is Mack Bolan, repeat, Mack Bolan. Refer to bulletin ten for full particulars and stand by for further instructions."

Bolan deactivated the monitors. They'd found his death medals. And they were, at this moment, reconstructing the details of a hard hit. Apparently this was some sort of quick reaction team, these cops, and they seemed to know precisely what they were doing.

They would know, now, that the war had moved to Seattle.

And—if this first light contact with the Seattle cops was any sort of indication—Bolan was going to have his hands full with these "soldiers of the same side."

It was food for thoughtful chewing. He chewed as he drove, not stopping until he'd cleared the top side of the city and reached the road to Richmond Beach. The night was turning gray and he was beginning to feel the effects of its activities

51

when he pulled over and went back to again check on the girl.

The breathing was easy and regular and she stirred to his touch, but the eyes remained closed.

Perhaps, he hoped, the fainting spell had simply turned into natural sleep.

Twenty minutes later he rolled the warwagon into her berth in the little camping park at the edge of Puget Sound—and this time when he went back, the girl was awake.

She had not moved, but her eyes were open, alert, and frightened.

She did not exactly smell like a rose, either.

"What is this?" she asked in a whispery voice. "Where am I? Who are you?"

"I'm the man with the gun," he replied gently. "This is my home. It has wheels. We're near Richmond Beach. There are neighbors all around. You can leave whenever you wish. But you shouldn't leave. Do you understand what has happened?"

It hit her like a flash flood, then—Bolan could see the memory of it washing across those terrified eyes. She shuddered and turned toward the wall.

He went to the shower and wet a towel with warm water, soaped it, and returned to the bunk.

"Put your legs out here," he commanded, in a gentle but no-nonsense tone.

"Wh-what?"

"They're caked with blood. Can't you smell it? Don't worry, it's not yours. But the drier it gets, the harder it comes off. Come on, the legs, let's have them."

"I—I can do it."

"Not if your stomach's as weak as your head, you can't. Just close your eyes and lie back. Look, doll, I carried you on my shoulder for half a mile. My hands already know every inch of you. Now give me the damn legs."

She did so without further protest—and she did not close her eyes. They remained on him, searching without expression, watching without comment as he removed the shoes and began the scrubdown. They were lovely eyes, blue with deep purple glints, perfect ovals, wide-spaced, intelligent, and growing very curious upon the man as he went on with his delicate labors.

Presently he showed her a gruff smile and told her, "I need more leg and less dress—unless you'd like to take over at this point."

"You're doing fine," the girl replied in a very small voice. She sat up and slid to the edge of the bunk, lowered her eyes, removed the dress, then lay back down. "I haven't been scrubbed like this since I was three," she said, sighing.

The strip had caught Bolan a bit off guard, and now that glowing young body in nothing but skimpy bra and even skimpier panties was raising hell with his manly instincts. He'd only meant that she should raise the dress a bit, not whisk the damn thing off. But she'd done it so naturally—with a total lack of self-consciousness yet not brazenly, either—just *natural*, yeah, as though she were removing a glove.

Bolan shrugged the instincts away and growled, "Turn over."

The dress had needed to come off, anyway. The machine gunner had obviously bled like hell. She looked as though she'd been lying in a pool of it.

He had to return twice to the shower to freshen the rub, and when he was finished the girl was glowing with more than cleanliness. The job had required some rather vigorous applications of the wet terry

53

cloth—and that rosy flesh had sustained quite a bit of stimulation.

She rolled over then, unfastened the bra, and pointed out some splatters to the front.

When Bolan finally stood away from that task, there simply was no way to shrug away the masculine emotions chugging through him.

And the girl was not helping a damn bit.

She whispered, "This is the most erotic experience of my life."

"Some life," he growled. "How long has it been? Eighteen years? Nineteen?"

"Twenty," she replied in that same soft little whisper. "And there have been experiences to relate to. This isn't 1940, you know."

"You can hit the shower now," he muttered, turning away from that implied invitation with nothing but sheer power of will. "It's a small tank, though. So just wet down, turn it off, soap down, quick rinse. Got it?"

She lay very still, hardly breathing. "You'd better show me."

"You'd better quit while you're ahead."

"Who's ahead? I feel like I'm running down a steep hill, plunging out of control. Show me how to work the shower."

Bolan growled, "Hell."

"Please. I really do feel very weak. I don't think I can move, by myself."

He sighed a resigned sigh of the damned, lifted her off the bunk, and carried her to the small shower enclosure, opened the door, set her inside on her feet.

The arms clung to his neck.

She wouldn't let go.

Gruffly, he told her, "You're not that damn weak."

"Yes I am," she insisted. "I'm afraid to bend over. I'll—how will I get my panties off?"

Bolan was a goner, and he knew it. It was no time for this sort of thing—and especially with a kid like this—but what the hell was a guy supposed to do?

He removed her arms from his neck and dropped to one knee at her feet to gently skin the flimsies from that delectable bottom—so full and charged and, he guessed, hurting. He remained there for a brief moment, gazing up at her. "You're in a lot of trouble, young lady," he said quietly.

"Yes, I know. So are you."

"I don't mean this."

"I do." She turned on the water and quickly adjusted the temperature, then handed him the soap. "You started it," she reminded him.

Half of Bolan was outside, half inside the enclosure. He straightened up and turned off the water, took the soap and began working a lather onto her thighs and belly.

She melted against him with a happy little sigh and huskily informed him, "You do have the touch. Get the back."

She was clutching him in a frontal embrace. He used "the touch" the full length of her spine and began working back toward the soft little shoulders. She shivered and said, "Lower, lower."

Bolan said, "For God's sake," and staggered out of there, whipped off his own sudsy clothing, and quickly rejoined.

She gave a whispery giggle and turned the water on again. "Your turn," she declared, seizing the soap.

And that was not all she seized.

Some time later they met the first penetrating rays of the sun curled limply together on the floor of the war room and gazing up through the one-way glass

55

into the murky skies—and Bolan spoke the first rational words since the shower stall.

"You're different," he told her.

"I am? How?"

He sighed. "I don't know how. Just different."

"You'll have to be more explicit than that," she said, teasing. "I have two legs, two arms, two boobs, and all the other usual equipment. What's different?"

"You," he said.

"Oh. Not my parts."

"Well they're okay, too. But there's something very . . . very natural about you. You know?"

She sighed. "Well that's no compliment. I belong to the natural generation."

He had no comment to that.

She went on, "We haven't even been introduced. No names. That's natural too, you know. For the now people, I mean."

"You're a now person?"

"Uh huh. Freedom, equality, all that."

"You're *Ms.* Webb, huh?"

"Oh! You *do* know my name!"

"Just that part. What's the rest?"

"Dianna."

"Goddess of love. It fits."

"Thanks. What are you? Thor, the god of war?"

He said, "You mean now or otherwise?"

She giggled. "You're very commanding. With a gun or . . . whatever."

"You remember that part, then."

"Oh sure. And by the way . . . thanks. I believe Tommy would really have used that gun on me. I mean, he's *insane!*"

A cold sensation floated along Bolan's nude frame. He asked, quietly, "You know that kid?"

"Oh sure. Tommy Rotten."

"Tommy what?"

"That's what the other men call him. I believe his real name is Rottino or something very Italian like that."

"Let's try something non-Italian," Bolan said. "How about Allan Nyeburg?"

"That's easy," she said with a sniff.

"How easy?"

"Very easy. Allan Nyeburg is my stepfather."

Oh sure. Natural, yeah.

If life was a game of craps, Bolan had just rolled a natural.

7: PRISONERS

Dianna Webb's mother had married Allan Nyeburg when the girl was fourteen. It was a marriage of desperation for Mrs. Webb—a suicide widow with plenty of social connections but little else, not even an insurance policy that would pay off. Nyeburg had seemed "nice," respectable, considerate—a young man "on his way" with plenty of financial stability already.

Dianna utterly despised him, always had.

"Inside that charming mask, he's a maniac," she told Bolan over breakfast, in that cool matter-of-fact tone which characterized her speech. "I'll tell you what sort of man Allan is. He's a compulsive skirt-chaser, and I mean *any* skirt. Always has a dozen women on the string. Every day without exception he has sex for lunch. I'm serious. A prostitute comes to the office at twelve sharp every day. Allan locks the door and they romp for an hour. Different girl every time. I guess it's some sort of compulsion. I know it is. In the evenings he sometimes sees two or three different women."

"Where's your mother through all this?"

"Suffering silently on the sidelines. The marriage was strictly an arrangement, sure, not a Hollywood type romance—but there's still such a thing as pride, you know. In my mother's circles, especially.

59

Imagine being married to a sex-driven—uh, what's the male equivalent to a nymphomaniac?"

"Lecher," Bolan said. "Unless he's really over the edge. Then a medical diagnosis could be satyriasis."

"Satyr," the girl said, nodding, "that's the word I was thinking of, and believe me, that's Allan. He *is* over the edge. My poor mother. Things like that don't remain quiet."

Bolan knew. He said, "Nothing does. Nyeburg has larger problems, though."

"He sure does," she quietly agreed. "I think he's really sick. He tried to put the move on me when I was fifteen. I was terrified. Didn't know how to handle a thing like that then. I mean he came on real crazy, tearing my clothes and everything. I stabbed him."

Bolan blinked his eyes at that and said, "Yeah?"

"Sure. Look, here's a kid who gets sick and practically goes into shock if someone pricks a finger. My father was . . . well . . . we found him in the bathtub. He, uh, slashed his wrists. Ever since, well —I just can't stand the sight of blood." She wrinkled her nose at a conflicting idea. "I don't know, maybe I'm over that now—after being baptized in the stuff last night. I honestly didn't feel anything when I woke up a while ago—except your presence."

Bolan nodded his head, understanding. He lit a cigarette and said, "So you once put a knife into your stepfather."

"Scissors," she corrected him. "And it wasn't all that big a deal. Of course I suppose I could have killed him. Obviously he thought so, anyway. It just caught him in the hand—and I guess it damaged me more than it did him. But it scared him, all right. And got me out of a bad situation."

"Would you do it again?" Bolan asked. "Now?"

"To him?" She mulled the idea briefly, then replied, "I suppose so, as a last resort. Actually, Allan does still try with me. I've learned how to handle the feints. And when he comes on real strong, I just tell him, 'Allan, I'll kill you.' He believes it." She sighed. "Well, you aren't interested in this dirty linen, are you?"

He showed her a faint smile and said, "Yes, I am. How does your mother feel about her husband's interest in her daughter?"

"She doesn't know. I'd never tell her a thing like that. The first time, when I stabbed him, Allan told everybody he'd accidentally cut himself with a letter opener. She knows about the others, though, the million and one faceless ones. She knows the sort of man Allan is. Driven."

"He's driven by more than sex," Bolan said with a sigh. "Aren't you curious about my interest in the guy?"

She smiled soberly. "Sure. When are you going to tell me about it? For that matter, when are you going to tell me about yourself?"

"You don't know about me?"

"Don't tell me that you're an undercover G-man."

Bolan chuckled. "Worse."

"Oh God, no! You couldn't be a *Narc!*"

It was a disturbing moment for Bolan, as were all such moments. Different individuals reacted in diverse ways to his unveiling. He'd assumed that the girl had known his identity since those first early moments at the warehouse—apparently she did not know but had accepted him on sheer face value. Soberly, he told her, "My name is Bolan."

"Bolan who?"

"Mack Bolan."

"Oh." She smiled. "Sure, it fits. It's a nice, Thor-type name. But what's the big deep secret?"

He'd hoped that the name alone would have told the tale. Certainly it was a name that could be recognized by anyone who read newspapers and magazines or watched television news shows.

She was saying, "I get the feeling I've heard that name before, haven't I?"

Bolan dug into the death trove and scattered medals across the breakfast table. "Some people know me by these," he said quietly.

She picked one up, inspected it with the eyes and fingers. "Hmmm. What in the world is it? Military, isn't it? What is it—an iron cross?" She laughed. "Are you a neo-Nazi?"

He shook his head, giving her the cool gaze. "The four-sided cross signifies, I guess, dedication and loyalty—something along that line. To me, it means judgment. The circles in the center represent a marksman's target—a bull's-eye. It's a marksman's medal."

The girl's eyes danced and her cheeks puffed with air. She released the trapped air with a Donald Duck squawk that sounded like "Wow!" Then she slid deeper into her chair to peer at him over crossed hands. "Sure," she said, reverting to the whispery voice. "I know you. I know all about you. You're a very tough guy, Mr. Bolan. Well I feel . . . gosh, I feel . . . why didn't you tell me? I mean, before . . . before . . . you know."

Indeed, Bolan knew. He said, "I assumed you knew. I identified myself when I stepped into that warehouse. You were there."

"Yes, but I—I guess I was thinking only about poor little me. I—I didn't . . ."

He asked, "Why were you there?"

"I was *dragged* there. So what am I to you? Is this . . . ?" Her eyes darted about the warwagon. "Is all this just . . . ? I mean, am I just a business matter?"

Gruffly, he replied, "Of course not. As long as you're here, though, you could be of help. I need to know what you were doing at that warehouse."

She sniffed and said, "Allan's bullycats dragged me down there. Made me show them where the stuff was."

"What stuff?"

She shook her head. "I don't know what it was. I never know. They're moving stuff into this country by the shipload. By air, too, I believe. But I don't know what they're doing with it."

He asked, "Why should you have to show them where it is? How would you know?"

She tossed her head and showed him a wry smile. "I didn't know until very lately, but I guess I'm their inside person. Allan got me this job with the exhibitor's council—Expo '74, you see. Stuff moving into the fair for exhibition enjoys duty-free status, you know."

"So?"

"So they've been moving this stuff in under Expo licenses for months. Smuggling, I guess—I don't know for sure. I work in the transportation section. It's my job to see that all the stuff coming into the Port of Seattle for storage pending exhibit is received and properly stored. This is a big thing, you know. It could be chaos if we couldn't keep track of the exhibit materials."

Bolan commented, "Yeah, I guess it would. So where does Nyeburg enter all this?"

"He got himself named as an advisor to the Expo board of governors. And he worked a deal with

63

several of the foreign exhibitors—to act as their agent in this country during all the complexities of getting this fair together. Spokane is—well, you know—it's not a very large city. This is all quite a giddy experience for them."

"Back to Nyeburg," Bolan prodded.

"Oh sure. Well he's a rat, that's all. I found out that half the stuff coming through this port with his name on it has nothing whatever to do with the fair. His bullycats have been coming down here and taking the stuff out of storage and spiriting it away somewhere. Then he expects me to dummy the records. I believe they're running narcotics, or something. I really do. I confronted Allan with my evidence last week. He laughed right in my face. Told me I'd better be a good little girl and keep those records straight. Otherwise he'd drag my mother through all the mud in Seattle."

"How would he do that?"

"He incorporated a legitimate company. It's called Pacific Northwest Associates. My mother is recorded as one of the officers."

Bolan said, "I see. I know about PNA. And he's right. He could implicate her. But you say they *dragged* you to the warehouse. Do you mean that literally?"

"I sure do. I told Allan to go to hell with his little crooked games. Told him I'd keep quiet about all the stuff in the past, but I was walking out of the rest of it."

"Good for you," Bolan said.

"Not good enough, I guess. They had this real hot shipment that they were all going crazy over. It was supposed to have arrived several days ago. Nobody could find it. But one of the darned warehousemen called, right in the middle of my little scene with Allan, to say that the shipment had been located. I had to tell him where to put it. Allan's gang of thieves went right down to get it, but the warehouse was closed. They broke in and still couldn't find it. So late last night, the bullycats came knocking at my door. They threw me in their car and hauled me down there to find the shipment for them. I played as dumb as they were for a while, then they got tough. The head cat called Allan from the warehouse and told him I wouldn't cooperate. Allan told him to slap me around some—those were the exact words that were relayed to me. The man didn't want to hit me, or so he said. But he told me that he would, rather than go back empty-handed."

The girl sighed. "I decided I wasn't all that heroic. I found the darned crate for them. I guess you know the rest."

Bolan did. He told her, "Your life isn't worth a nickel right now."

Fear flickered in those cool eyes but the voice was casual as she asked, "Why not? I gave them what they wanted."

"You also *saw* what they wanted," he pointed out. "Worse, you can tie it all back to Nyeburg—and puncture his claim of ignorance."

"I didn't see inside those crates," the girl protested.

"That's the least consideration now," Bolan told her. "The police know, now, and you—dear heart—are a very vulnerable spot in your stepfather's armor. The stakes are too high in this game, Dianna. Nyeburg won't hesitate for a moment to take you out of play. He has probably been planning it since the moment you began to oppose him."

That shook her. She mused, "I believe he would."

"Sure he would. This is a mob operation. And not just a local mob. Nyeburg is fronting a worldwide

65

crime syndicate. Whatever they're up to here, you can believe they have millions invested and a whole world to gain. They'd snuff you like a fly at a picnic table."

"That sounds pretty far out," the girl said, still shaken but trying to argue the point. "Allan? Head of a James Bond bunch of heavies?"

"He's not the head, he's just the face. And these guys have probably never heard of James Bond. In the movies, Dianna, everybody gets up and has a drink together when the shooting is over. This bunch plays for keeps. Nobody gets up when the shooting is over."

"Yes," she agreed, shuddering, evidently remembering the gunplay of a few hours earlier. "I never realized that such . . . *awful* things happen to a person when—when they get shot like that. It's like an explosion, inside of them. I mean *gushing* and . . . and . . ."

"That it is," Bolan said, sighing. "Look, Dianna—I'm not just trying to scare you, but I do have to impress upon you the very grave nature of your predicament. I don't want you running back to Nyeburg with a pair of scissors in your hand. It's a different game now. You have to understand that."

"Yes, I—I'll go to the police," she whispered. "Mother will just have to—God! She's in as much danger as I am!"

Bolan shook his head. "Not yet. But you can't go to the cops, for another reason."

"I will! I'll just—"

"No, Dianna."

"No?"

"It would increase your visibility ten-fold. Even if you requested protective confinement, you could still be had. Many contractees have died while

66

neatly penned up in a jail cell, or in a hotel room under police guard."

The girl shuddered. "Contractee?"

He had to level with her. "Yeah. I'll give you odds at a million to one that your name is already on a death contract."

"Oh!"

"Scary, isn't it?"

"Yes. What can I do?"

"Stay low. Don't go near anywhere you've ever been before. Contact no one—not by phone or otherwise. Don't use any credit cards. Don't write any checks. Don't use your driver's license or social security card. Don't drive any vehicle that could be traced back to you. Change your whole life-style, clothing, everything. Even the color of your hair."

"I'm a free citizen of a free country!" she said defiantly, angered now.

"So are the others," he pointed out. "They're free to kill. You're free to die."

"I just can't believe this," she muttered angrily.

"You'd better. I've been believing it for a long time now, Dianna. I remain alive. You can, too, by believing—and acting accordingly."

"My God," she said miserably.

"It may not have to last long. If I can break the thing up, quick and hard, there'll be no contracts left for anybody."

"That's your thing, isn't it," she said.

He nodded his head. "It is."

The full import of the situation was settling in on the girl. "But where would I go?" she cried. "I don't know where to start! I even left my purse—I don't have a dime! How do I . . . ?"

Bolan sighed and broke contact with those

67

troubled eyes. "Okay," he said tiredly. "You do have one option. But it could be even more dangerous than the other."

"Options? I'll take them," she said. "Besides, what could be more dangerous?"

"Me," he said quietly.

"Huh?"

"You can stay here a while. It's safe, for the moment. But everybody with a gun in this town will be looking for me. You could find yourself in the middle of a very hot war, which is contractee times a hundred. Also, the same conditions will apply. You're to show yourself to no one. You'll be a prisoner of this van."

Those eyes were beginning to dance again. She said, "Prisoner, eh?"

"Prisoner at large," he replied, smiling soberly.

"How about prisoner of love? Think we could work in something along those lines?"

"Don't bet on it," he told her gruffly. "I'll be a very busy soldier from here on."

"But I will bet," she said with a whispery laugh. "What do I have to lose? I like your option, Mr. Bolan. War and all, I like it very much. But you really didn't have to scare the pants off of me just to—"

She noted the glint of despair in Bolan's eyes and cut herself off with a grimace.

"Hey, I'm sorry. Really. I was just clowning. I'm really sorry. I didn't mean that. It really is a pretty tough deal, isn't it? I mean, *your* deal. You're a prisoner, too, aren't you? Of your own war."

"It's pretty tough," Bolan admitted. "But I dealt the hand, Dianna. It's my game. Make no mistake about that. Don't start building romantic fantasies about what a poor, misunderstood soul I am. It's my game. And I play for keeps, too. It's *my* game."

She shivered and reached for him.

"It's mine, too—now," she whispered.

8: DOMINO

It was raining as it can only in Seattle. A brooding nimbostratus lay over the entire coastal region, sending down a steady torrent which had not let up for two drenching hours. Bolan could have closed his eyes and imagined that he was back in 'Nam during monsoon—except for that clammy chill settling into his bones.

A cape-style raincoat had kept him relatively dry from the shoulders down to just above the ankles— and the rain itself, heavy enough to substantially restrict visibility, provided pretty good cover for a surveillance mission. But that was about all the good that could be said of the situation. His feet were awash and the persistent moisture of nature's universal solvent had discovered pathways into the cape and down his neck.

The time was two o'clock in the afternoon; the place, just outside the small suburban office building that housed the headquarters of Pacific Northwest Associates—Nyeburg's outfit.

Bolan had been on station since noon, positioned for surveillance of both entrances to the building. PNA was the only occupant. Dianna Webb had sketched the interior layout for him; he knew the building as well, probably, as anyone who'd ever been in there. It was a small, squarish structure—

71

single story. Built originally to serve as a branch bank, it sat off to the side of the parking lot for a large shopping center. A drive-up window remained in service—Dianna explaining that Nyeburg conducted "quite a bit" of business via that handy device.

No "business" had been conducted there during the past two hours. Bolan had abandoned his vehicle—a rented Fairlane—ten minutes into the stakeout, electing to take the weather in exchange for a reliable surveillance.

But nothing had moved in or out of that building for two hours, and Bolan was beginning to wonder. He stepped into a phone booth, fed in a dime, and called the cops.

He got a switchboard operator.

He asked her, "Do you have a public information officer on duty?"

She asked him, "Who's calling, please?"

"Peterson, United News."

"One minute, sir."

Bolan lit a soggy cigarette and marked twenty seconds by his watch before the operator returned. "Thank you for waiting, sir. The press liaison Captain Parris, will take the call. One moment, please."

Two clicks later, Bolan was talking to his man.

He said, "Afternoon, Captain. Just got off the plane from L.A. What's your principal resource up here? Water?"

The guy chuckled. "You came in with the rains, Mr. Peterson. Sure you didn't bring it up with you?"

"No way," Bolan replied cordially. "We need it all down there, to strain the smog. I brought a lot of excitement, though. We heard about your Executioner war. I drew the stick for combat correspondent."

"You should have called ahead," the Captain said, still amiable. "Maybe I could have saved you a trip. Uh, uh, dammit—I realize I should know your whole name, but I talk to a lot of—"

"Harry—Harry Peterson, United News Service."

"Oh sure, sure—heard that name a lot, of course. All to your credit."

That was nice. Bolan hadn't. He told the PLO, "I'll be coming right into town but thought I'd check into a hotel first if nothing really electrifying is happening at the moment."

"Electrifying, no. Like I said, I could probably have saved you the trip. You and about a hundred more of your fellows who are presently pacing the corridors outside here right now."

"You're saying there's no war?"

"Well . . . it's not definite either way. That's what we're saying for quotes."

"Why are you saying that? Word came out of here this morning early that—"

"First and foremost, uh Harry, there has been but a single strike. That isn't like Bolan. I mean, it's been—what? Almost twelve hours? Usually by this time the guy would have the whole town reeling. Right? Well, nothing's reeling, Harry. Then, too— Seattle's a pretty clean town."

Bolan laughed into the transmitter.

"No, really. We've cleaned up the little embarrassments we had in the past. It was all penny-ante stuff, anyway. There's no substantial organized crime activity in the area. Not the sort of stuff to bring Bolan onto the scene."

Bolan/Peterson chuckled and said, "You're sure of that, eh?"

"As sure as anyone can ever be."

"Well I'm interested in the Expo '74 angle."

73

The guy sighed. "So's everybody else. Look, Harry, we'd appreciate it if you boys would play down that angle. They're having enough trouble getting this thing launched without having to combat an avalanche of rumors that—"

"Sure, I understand. But there does seem to be a connection. If the mob isn't into it, who is? Who's smuggling the guns?"

"We're investigating, uh—the federal boys, of course, that's their prime jurisdiction. We're more interested in—"

"What about Nyeburg?"

"Unfortunate, very unfortunate."

"What is?" Bolan really wanted to know.

"Nyeburg is a respected businessman in this state. We got our tit in a ringer over that damn press release this morning. Nyeburg is not involved in any way. Evidently someone knew that he was an Expo official, authorized to receive foreign exhibits. It made a good cover—but very unfortunate for Nyeburg. We're issuing a statement clearing him of any suspicion in the matter."

"Sure you're not being premature again?"

"Sure we're sure."

"I'd wait if I were you."

"Uh, look, Harry—I'm going overboard with all you people in the interests of, uh, factual reporting. My office is prepared to cooperate with the media in every way possible. But you can't do our work for us, you know."

"I can try," Bolan replied. "I do think——"

"Come on in, we'll split a gallon of coffee. You'll have plenty of company. I've got media people out the ass around here. Come on in."

The voice went icy as Bolan told the genial captain, "Can't. I've got to go hit Nyeburg."

"What?"

"Well if you guys aren't, that leaves only me."

"What? What are you—say! What the hell is this!"

"This is Bolan. Sorry for the little masquerade, but I needed the poop. Don't release that statement on Nyeburg, it will bounce. The guy's guilty as sin. I'm going to take him. Stay loose, Captain."

Bolan hung up to a dead silence, studied his fingertips thoughtfully for a brief moment, then stepped outside to rejoin the downpour.

Even if the PLO should take it serious and alert the hard cops, he figured it would take a while to get a response going.

He moved directly across the rainwashed parking lot, pausing halfway across to take note of the fact that it was largely deserted—due, perhaps, to the bad weather—formulating a quick plan to be played by ear with both fingers crossed all the way. He went on to the PNA office and stepped inside. It no longer looked like a banking substation in there. Interior modifications had resulted in a small reception room separated from an outer office by a low, wrought-iron railing. A leather couch and a couple of chairs were the chief decor; beyond the railing, two desks and a couple of file cabinets; beyond there, closed doors to a pair of inner offices; at the far end of the reception area, a rear exit.

Two attractive young women, a blonde and a brunette—punching bags, probably, for a lecherous boss—were in a coffee klatch at the desks, snickering over something and obviously having a good time. Both looked up at Bolan's entrance but neither made a move toward greeting him. The blonde glared distastefully at the moisture dripping from his cape, then turned away.

He locked the door and turned the "closed" sign

75

into position, then sloshed on to the railing and told the girls, "Okay, you're closed. Hurry!"

Both women merely stared at him, faces blank.

He opened the gate and held it for them. "Go on. Hurry. Didn't you get the flash? You got about thirty seconds to evacuate this joint."

The blonde leapt to her feet and gasped, "What?"

"Methane gas escaping," Bolan explained. "Come on, we're clearing the whole area. Anybody else in here?"

The blonde staggered bug-eyed toward her purse, stuttering and pointing toward the closed door behind her. The other girl was already moving toward that door. Bolan intercepted her and pulled her back. "Go on," he commanded. "I'll get them. Go out the back. Get in your cars and get moving. Head south."

The women made a dash for the rear door.

Bolan tried the door to the inner office and found it locked. He kicked it open and moved in quickly, the silent Beretta in hand and ready beneath the cape.

Tommy Rotten sat at a small desk with a *Penthouse* magazine spread before him on the desk. Surprised eyes lifted to the imposing figure in the glistening cape. He yelped, "What is—?" and cut it off there, his own gaze arrested by the death stare in those other, icy eyes. Recognition flared, then, and he groaned, "Oh Jesus!"

"Where's Nyeburg?"

"Jesus I don't know!"

Bolan squeezed off a whispering round from beneath the cape. It plowed through the magazine at dead center between the youth's outspread hands and thwacked on into the wood beneath.

The kid jumped a foot off the chair and the hands leapt skyward.

"Honest I don't know!" he yelled. "Hey, I ain't armed!"

"Nyeburg!" Bolan insisted.

"He didn't come in! Didn't even call! I don't know nothing!"

All the yelling brought someone who might know, though. She was a lady all the way, still quite lovely in a mature fashion, a senior edition of Dianna Webb as she stepped quietly in from the adjoining office. Cool eyes swept from the quaking youth to the tall man in the other doorway. The voice even sounded like Dianna's as she inquired, "What is going on here?"

"I'm looking for your husband," Bolan replied, just as coolly.

"He's out of town. Tommy, sit down."

Bolan said, "He stands! Open that door all the way, Mrs. Nyeburg, and come on in here."

Those cool eyes faltered a bit. She said, "I see," and did as she was told.

Bolan stepped past her and took a quick look into the other office. A heavy vault occupied one entire wall—a holdover, perhaps, from branch banking.

Bolan told the lady, "You'll have to open the vault."

She replied, "What if I refuse? Will you shoot me?"

He said, "No. But I might take another shot at the kid."

"I'll open it. But you won't find Mr. Nyeburg in there."

"Maybe I'll find his tracks, though," Bolan said, smiling despite himself. She was a cool lady. "Do it," he said, still smiling faintly.

Tommy Rotten gasped, "Do it, please, Mrs. Nyeburg. This guy is Mack Bolan. The Executioner. You know. Do it, please!"

Yes, she knew. She had already known. As she returned to the other office, she told Bolan, "The police sketches on television don't do you justice, Mr. Bolan. You look twice as mean, in person."

He said, "Win some, lose some."

Tommy Rotten was accorded a wag of the head. The boy moved quickly to follow the woman. Bolan stepped in behind them and closed the door.

As Mrs. Nyeburg worked on the vault, Bolan worked on the boy.

"Are you a made man, Tommy?"

"No sir, not yet."

"Who's your sponsor?"

"Sir?"

"Your connection—who's sponsoring you?"

"Danny Trinity."

"Too bad. You've lost a sponsor."

"Yessir, I been wondering. I mean, I lost everybody."

"Related?"

"Sir?"

"Were you related to Danny Trinity?"

"Yessir, we're cousins."

"Were."

"Yessir. We were."

"How old are you?"

"Eighteen."

"How long you been connected?"

"Just, uh, since we come out here."

"From the Bronx."

"Yessir, from the Bronx and Staten Island. Hey, I never done nothing like this before."

"What have you done?"

"Sir? Nothing! I ain't done nothing! I just got outta school."

"You should have stayed, Tommy."

"Yessir."

"You know Tony Vale?"

"A little. He's Danny's boss."

"Was. Danny's dead. Remember?"

"Yessir."

"You like the guy?"

"Tony? No sir."

"Feel like working for him some day?"

"No sir."

"You have a car here?"

"Yessir. The Vega parked just outside."

"Okay. Get in that Vega. Take off. Don't look back and don't come back. Next time I see you, Tommy, I'll take you. Don't let me see you again."

"Yessir. I appreciate—I promise—you won't never see me again."

"Before you go, tell the lady here all about it."

"Sir?"

"Tell the lady why you're here."

The vault stood open. Mrs. Nyeburg had been staring at the youth with a perplexed frown. He looked toward her and his eyes fell. He stared at the floor and told her, "Mrs. Nyeburg, I been working for the organization—the mob, you know, the Mafia. We come out here on a special detail to back up your husband. He's mob, too."

She said, coolly, "I see."

Bolan said, "Okay, Tommy, take off. Use the back door."

The boy left, eyes downcast.

Bolan waited until he heard the click of the rear door, then he told the lady, "You married a rat, Mrs. Nyeburg."

She merely sighed.

"That boy who just walked out of here was holding a gun at your daughter's head a few hours ago. He was ready to shoot her. I believe he was authorized to do so. By your husband."

That jarred the lady. The eyes flared then settled down again as she asked, "Do you know where she is now? I've been worried sick."

Bolan told her, "I could trade with you—your daughter for your husband—but that would be dishonest. She's safe and well where she is. No thanks to good old Allan, though. I have good reason to believe that he has ordered her death."

She really reacted to that one. Her legs must have suddenly gone weak. She sagged onto a desk and passed a hand across her brow. "I have been stupid," she whispered. "*Stupid!*"

"You've suspected, haven't you?"

"I've been wondering."

"Time to stop wondering, Mrs. Nyeburg." Bolan moved to the vault and took a look inside. There wasn't much. A few stacks of official-looking papers, a couple of ledgers, a locked metal box. He scooped the whole works into a stack and asked the lady, "You want to come with me?"

"Where?"

"I'll take you to Dianna."

She stood up, working at her emotions, cinching them in.

Bolan put an arm about her shoulders and led her out.

As he was draping a raincoat over her, she swiped away a tear and said, "Did I say 'mean,' Mr. Bolan? You don't look mean. You look beautiful."

Sure. He was a beautiful bastard. Knocking over

dominoes, and she simply happened to be at the head of the line. But there was, he reminded himself, no morality in a holy war.

"Stay hard, Mrs. Nyeburg," he muttered.

9: DRUMS

Bolan had to believe that the lady was leveling with him. She had neither seen nor heard from Allan Nyeburg since he "ran out of the house" at about six o'clock that morning. He had not told her where he was going or when she could expect him back.

He'd made several phone calls earlier, from their bedroom, after being awakened by a call which "did not last thirty seconds."

Her husband had been very nervous and excited. One of his calls was long distance, direct-dialed; she could tell this by the long combination of digits. His voice during that conversation had been low, guarded, urgent. She understood none of it. That conversation lasted about five minutes. Then he made several local calls, all short, all very urgent in tone. Then he got out of bed, dressed hurriedly, and left without breakfast or even coffee.

And, yes, she'd been worried.

Dianna had been involved in some sort of intrigue with Allan's business for several weeks—all of which was very mysterious and quietly alarming for the mother. She had called Dianna's apartment at six thirty and every fifteen minutes thereafter until past eight o'clock. Then she'd gone to the office and awaited word. Tommy Rentino came in at ten o'clock, sheepish and taciturn—insisting that he'd seen neither Dianna nor Nyeburg since early the preceding evening. Tommy had been, she'd thought, a sort of messenger boy and special courier for her husband. Under close questioning by Mrs. Nyeburg, the boy had admitted that "something had gone sour"—but he could not or would not explain further.

At eleven thirty, she turned on a small portable television in her office to catch the midday news—fearful and halfway expecting to hear something "grisly" concerning her husband's crisis. What she caught was a special program aired by the local affiliate, a repeat of a network news special of a few weeks earlier, chronicling the life and wars of one Mack Bolan—with local reportage of the events of the early morning hours in Seattle.

Then she'd really become worried.

She'd tried reaching both Nyeburg and her daughter by telephone at every conceivable location—drawing a blank, of course, each time.

By the time Mack Bolan strode into her offices, she was seriously contemplating calling the police with a missing persons report.

Bolan stopped off at a small variety store on the way to Richmond Beach and picked up a few items. A mile from the warwagon, he gave Margaret Nyeburg a pair of dark eyeshades and asked her to put them on, explaining simply that he did not wish her burdened with information she'd be better off without. She complied without complaint.

He removed the shades himself when she stepped inside the warwagon. Mother and daughter had a noisy and tearful reunion while Bolan went out and attached the rented car to a tow bar at the rear of the larger vehicle.

Inside again, he gave the ladies his purchases from the variety store—bluejeans and flannel shirts, deck-shoes, bandannas for the hair—and told them what to do with them.

While they changed, he sent the warwagon cruising north along the coast to a small beach house several miles along. This was his "rear base," rented shortly after his arrival in the area and not used until this moment. The house was semi-isolated, fully stocked with foodstuffs and other necessities adequate for a week-long stay, snug, secure. Bolan would have put his own kid in there.

He told the ladies, "There's no phone. Which is good—there won't be the temptation to start calling around for news. There's a radio—use that, instead. I want you to stay here and keep out of sight until you hear different from me personally. Your lives are now in your own hands. Keep it that way."

He went out then, and the younger lady followed him onto the porch. "So it's Prisoner of Mom," she said with a wry smile. "What's the matter—can't take the heat?"

He replied, "We'll take up that question later. Love and death don't make a very winning combination, Dianna." He smiled. "I'll give you a chance to eat those words. Later."

She smiled back and said, "Sure."

"Watch her," Bolan cautioned, referring to the mother. "She didn't get the baptism you did. Make sure she doesn't have movie ideas about blood and guts."

The girl winced. She asked, "What are you going to do to Allan?"

Bolan shrugged. "The guy is wearing the mark of the beast. I didn't put it there. He did."

"Well sure, but . . ." She tossed a quick glance through the open doorway. "She couldn't possibly love the man, Thor. But they *have* been man and wife for over six years. I-I just . . . don't judge him too harshly."

Bolan frowned as he told the girl, "I don't judge, Dianna. I don't even condemn. I just read the marks, and I fulfill. These guys are their own judge and their own jury. Hell I'm just the executioner."

"That's tough, oh that's tough," she argued quietly. "Wish I could be that tough, but I'm not. Neither is my mother. Don't—please don't . . ."

Tough, sure. Bolan's dreams were haunted by the wraiths of weeping widows.

"No promises," he said gruffly. "But I will play it by the ear. If the fates should smile on Allan, okay. If not . . ."

She said, very quietly and almost conspiratorially, "You know, it's funny—I'm not the least little worried about *you*. You're so—so damn *awesome*. What are you, Thor Bolan? What makes you tick?"

The senior version edged through the doorway at that moment to officially join the conversation. Margaret Nyeburg said, "If you'd been watching television this morning, Dy, you wouldn't have to ask that. Go on, Mr. Bolan. Do what you must do. I'm sorry, yes, I have been listening. Don't risk one of your fingers for the sake of Allan Nyeburg."

Bolan gave them both a flash of warm blue eyes and a quiet farewell.

That was a mighty cool lady back there, he was thinking as he wheeled the warwagon back toward town. Some day, if she was damn lucky, the junior miss would be just as cool—and as beautiful.

Nyeburg really had to be some kind of sick dude—to shit on a woman like that. On *women* like that.

Bolan, however, was no doctor. He did not cure, he eradicated. This was his focus. To change focus

86

would be to dilute the effect. And the "effect" was all he had going.

At that moment, he was "going" for Allan Nyeburg. With the active assistance of the man's wife. The lady had given Bolan a list of addresses and phone numbers. They pertained to Nyeburg's "illness."

If you're looking for a junkie, watch the pushers. Bolan was off to watch the pimps.

At the far side of the country, an agitated young man with hat pulled low over his eyes was stepping into an official vehicle at the national airport in Washington, D.C. He was the object of the most closely guarded government secret since the Manhattan Project. His name was Leo Turrin. He was ranking boss of the Pittsfield arm of a larger Massachusetts crime family. He was a popular and "coming" young "executive" in the far-flung empire of *la Cosa Nostra*, enjoying the confidence and respect of the ruling council as well as the general rank and file. The secret was that he was also *Sticker* —the code name for the most sensitive government agent in the undercover ranks.

Only one man in Washington knew the true identity of Sticker. That man was Harold Brognola, the top official in the government's anti-crime program. Curiously enough, Brognola was also the official charged with the responsibility to "stop Mack Bolan."

Curious, because these two men were the closest friends Mack Bolan had in the world. It had been largely through Bolan's activities that Turrin rose so swiftly through Mafia ranks. And it had been largely through Bolan's mob-busting heroics that Hal Brognola had become such an impressive figure on

87

the Washington scene. Both of these men privately acknowledged their debts to Mack Bolan even while discounting his own debts to them—which were many.

It was a rare occasion for Turrin and Brognola to make direct, personal contact—and very risky. Brognola was a bit testy, in fact, as Turrin slid into the car beside him. "What's the panic?" he growled.

They shook hands as Turrin growled back, "No panic and stop worrying. I'm well covered. The boys think I have a woman stashed down here. You are kinda cute, at that, you know."

Brognola cussed under his breath. "Maybe you're covered but I'm not so sure I am. This town has gone insane, Leo. Pure crazy. Nobody trusts anybody. I go over this vehicle with a de-bugger before every use. I'm afraid to make love to my wife in my own bed, except in whispers. The whole town is paranoid."

"Well, it's your White House," Turrin commented with a droll smile. "Hell, I live with that stuff forever. It's about time you boys in Washington took some of the heat."

The official chuckled drily. "It's getting so you can't tell the players without a scorecard, Leo. Seriously. I'm worried sick. This country could topple."

"It's that serious?"

"It is. I wish I could tell you—no I don't. I wouldn't burden anyone with that. Besides you have problems enough of your own. Now, dammit, what's so urgent?"

"I just came out of a meeting with the old men in New York. Ducked out to La Guardia and hopped the commuter right down, zip zip. Marvelous age, isn't it."

"Full council?"

"Yeah. In spades."

"Since when do they let you into the councils?"

"Since today. Special invitation. I'm the Bolan expert, you know."

"Ah hell, not that again. Seattle, eh?"

"Yeah. Hal, they're fielding a special killer force to go get that guy."

Brognola grimaced. "I quit worrying about Mack Bolan a long time ago. They've sent forces out before. Anyway—our Seattle office says there's some question that Bolan is even there. Have you heard from the guy?"

"Not since New Orleans," Turrin said. "But he's there, all right."

"Why? Nothing else is there, not that I've been able to ascertain. Except for a few small nickel and dime operations that Bolan wouldn't wipe his feet on."

"That's what I thought, too," Turrin replied. "But . . ."

"But what?"

"Well, hell. You know how the mob feels about Mack Bolan. They'd rather have him than Canada. I mean, they fantasize fucking his bleeding head instead of hot twats. They'd spend anything and do anything to get a good shot at the guy. And, like you say, they've sent forces before. But, Hal . . . these old men are pole-vaulting all over the offices up there right now, have been all day. I kept expecting Augie to go into relapse, he's so nuts over this thing. I mean they're frothing at their collective mouths. They're scared to death, I'll tell you. This isn't just a usual hate-Bolan week. They're really shook up."

"Over *what*?"

"Hell, that's what I couldn't learn. All I know is that something big—something superfragile big is about to happen out there in Seattle. And they're losing their minds over the Bolan presence."

"That's why you came down?"

"That's why. I've been ordered out there."

Brognola sighed. "How many guns you taking?"

"Just my usual crew. The killer force is being put together from St. Louis, Denver, Phoenix, and Frisco. Two hundred—now get this—T-W-O hundred guns. The meanest boys in the west. I don't have any command. I'm just there, as an advisor, strategist. Guy by the name of Franciscus will be the top gun. Heard of him?"

Brognola worriedly shook his head.

"Me either. He's not a made man, either. Independent contractor. Ex-soldier, with combat credentials. The old men were heh-hehing all over the joint, rubbing their hands in anticipation and congratulating each other over the pickup on this guy. They seem to think he'll be a match for Bolan's combat M. O. But there's something else about this guy that . . ."

"Yeah, what? Don't stop there."

"The guy's already in Seattle."

"So?"

"So he's *been* there, since before Bolan showed. That's too much for mere coincidence. Isn't it? I think . . . Hal, I believe Franciscus was already there—for the other thing, the big thing whatever it is. And somehow it all ties in to . . ."

"To what?"

"Hell, I don't know. How do you express gut hunches? This Franciscus is a military type. He was a captain of infantry, brushfire forces. And he's not made. So what the hell were they setting up for that guy in Seattle? Of all damned places, *Seattle!*"

Brognola's usually impassive face had settled into

grim lines. "Treasury is looking into the Seattle thing, of course," he said quietly. "There were two hundred automatic weapons discovered in that warehouse out there this morning. So far it's being handled as a routine case of illegal trafficking in restricted weapons. But . . . now you say they're fielding two hundred *gunners*."

"Could that be a coincidence?"

"I'd hate to bet on it," the official replied with a worried smile. "What the hell do you think they're doing?"

"I've thought of a million things, all too crazy. I don't know, Hal. I *do* know how hard it is to scrape up two hundred good gunners on a moment's notice. If the weapons were already there, and if the two hundred boys were already stashed around waiting for the call—then by God I'd punch the umpire before I'd settle for a coincidence call."

"You're right. And they couldn't have been primed and waiting for Bolan to show. That's too ridiculous."

"Aw no," the undercover man said quickly. "I told you, the old men are half out of their minds because the guy *did* show."

"Do you think those wiseguys were already putting together a paramilitary force? Are you saying that Bolan tumbled to it, and that's why he's there?"

Turrin gave a heavy sigh and cracked his knuckles through a long silence. Presently he replied, "Like I said, I haven't talked to the Sarge since New Orleans. I don't know what the hell he's onto. But I'd bet my life on this much. He's onto *something*, or he wouldn't be romping. And the old men wouldn't be stomping."

"Hell, I guess I'd getter get out there, too," Brognola decided.

"My plane leaves in an hour."

"So will mine," the official said. "I'll take fifty marshals. Maybe I can scrounge up another fifty when I get out there. Where will you be?"

"I'll be at the best hotel they have. Leave messages for Joseph Petrillo."

"Fine. You'll know where to reach me."

Turrin chuckled without humor. "Sure you can afford to leave Washington behind for a few days?"

"Hell, I'm traveling from one to the other, the city to the state."

"Yeah," Turrin said, "but what a contrast in smells, eh?"

"We'll see," said the Justice Department official.

"Sure," Turrin replied. "I guess we'll see plenty."

They would.

Already, the war drums were throbbing throughout the Pacific Northwest.

10: THE BREW

Bolan moved his base camp to a commercial camp-
ground on the eastern approaches to the city. There
he changed clothes and snacked while going through
the stuff from Nyeburg's vault. The only thing of any
immediate interest there was a ledger with some
rather cryptic notations, and the lockbox—which
contained twenty thousand dollars in crisp new $100
bills.

He dropped half of the money into his warchest
and deposited the rest in his coat pocket, stowed the
other stuff, and drove the Fairlane into Seattle.

It was six o'clock when he hit town. The rain
had stopped but the skies continued to threaten and
were bringing on a premature nightfall.

He scored on his first stop, which had been carefully selected from the list of possibilities. It was a
small "models and escorts" agency located in the
hotel district. Bolan could smell a guy like Nyeburg
all over that joint.

The guy at the desk was about fifty, fat, balding,
with a perpetual smile—and he looked as though
he had perhaps grown into the chair.

Bolan placed a shiny new hundred in front of the
guy and said, "Hi."

"Hi," grinning boy replied. "What's that for?"

"That's for you," Bolan said, matching the smile.

93

"Yeah?"

"Sure. I got nine more just like it to say that you're the man for me."

"Whatta you got—a sales convention?" The guy snickered. "Or do you just want to die happy."

"Doesn't everybody?" Bolan kept right on smiling as he counted off nine more bills and asked the guy, "What will that get?"

"Any damn thing you want," said laughing boy.

"I want a guy with about a two hundred dollar a day habit."

"Huh?"

"Guy about forty. Never won a beauty contest but not too horrible, I guess, as Johns go. Pretty wealthy. Likes 'em for lunch, likes 'em for dinner, and now and then for a midnight snack. I think you've been servicing the guy. I'm trying to locate him."

The smile hung in there but the spirit didn't. "Hey now *wait* a *minute* there. I don't know what you're saying and I don't want any. I get involved in nothing, bud, *nothing*."

"You'd better get involved in this, bud. My way or trouble's way."

Eyes that had seen everything and every kind of guy were now sizing up the Executioner. "You're not a cop, huh."

"Course not. But I want the guy and I want him tonight." Bolan's smile outdid itself. "Save us all a lot of trouble. Make yourself a thousand bucks in the bargain."

The fat man carefully picked up the money. "I think I know the guy."

"You sent him somebody today. Right?"

"Sure. Every day. With this guy, it's a constantly revolving door. I sent him something an hour ago."

94

Bolan placed his warbook on the desk and opened it to a clean page. "Put the address there."

The guy did so, in huge block print. Then he asked Bolan, "You know about where that is?"

Bolan glanced at the book and replied, "Not exactly."

"I figured you're not from here. Who is, these days, eh?" He sighed. "It cost my client twenty bucks extra for cab fare. It's across Lake Washington on I-90 East. Take the *first* offramp to Lake Sammamish. Stop at a gas station out there and ask for directions. It's a wooded area. You get lost easy."

"He get service out there regularly?" Bolan idly wondered.

"Out there? Naw. Once or twice before this, maybe. When this guy needs, he *needs*. He don't care where he is. You're right—that bit about lunch. I send 'em to his office—isn't that rich. Every man's fantasy—a broad under the desk keeping him alert during the boring daily routine."

"Not every guy can afford to indulge that fantasy," Bolan said.

"This one can. You said two hundred a day? Try three and four, some days."

Everybody loved to gossip.

Bolan said, "That's worse than smack."

"Sure it is. On that much smack, he'd be dead long ago. Frankly, I don't get it. I even asked the girls what the *hell* he does with 'em. He *screws* 'em, that's what. Sure, sometimes a half a dozen different girls the same day. I still can't believe it. I wish one of those sex surveyors would come around and survey *me*. Boy, what I could tell 'em."

"You paying protection?"

"Aw no, no. We keep a low profile, nobody bothers

us. No open solicitation, no street walkers. Good girls, clean and all."

"Nobody's tried to muscle you?"

"Aw hell, no. This is a quiet town. Where you from?"

"East," Bolan said. "People like you don't have a chance there. The mob runs it all."

"Oh well, hey, we've got no mob *here*." The guy was getting nervous. "Don't uh, don't get any ideas, friend. I mean, if you're thinking of some little muscle action on your own. You wouldn't last a day. I said I wasn't *paying* protection. That doesn't mean I don't *have* it."

"Relax," Bolan said. "I was just wondering if this superjohn of yours was actually *paying* or . . ."

"Oh hell, he pays. Cash on the line."

Bolan thanked the guy and got out of there.

He did not particularly like the feel of the situation. His mind nibbled briefly at the idea of *set-up* but discarded it as too unlikely.

As for the Lake Sammamish area, it rang out okay. It fit the situation. Good place for a quiet pad where a guy could get away from it all when the need was there. Margaret Nyeburg, if she'd come entirely clean, did not know of such a place. Which made the ring even cleaner.

Bolan had early-on discarded the thought that Nyeburg may have gone to the island. It was out of his league, totally out of reach. Nyeburg was a *face*, not a head—and it mattered not at all that his face officially owned the place.

Nyeburg wasn't even made. Bolan's chief interest in the guy lay in the "domino chain" idea. He had to spark a chain reaction somewhere. Nyeburg seemed the likeliest domino in the line.

The guy had wasted no time getting out of sight.

Margaret had said that he'd received this early morning call which "lasted no more than thirty seconds."

Tommy Rotten didn't make that call; the kid couldn't coherently say that much in that space of time—certainly not enough to send Nyeburg in panic to the men in New York, which is immediately what he did—that five minute long distance conference.

A few minutes later, the guy was running out of his house in panic.

So who called and tipped him in the first place, if not the sole survivor of the gunfight?

Someone with clout. Clout enough to influence a police investigation. Clout enough to put the brakes on a Bolan-alert which would put the whole town in arms.

Sure.

The mob never moved into virgin territory, not in force, without a bit of advance legal insurance. Somebody in Seattle was greasing the way. Allan Nyeburg probably knew who that somebody was— or, at least, he would know the next man in the chain, the next layer of responsibility.

Bolan needed desperately to tip that domino.

A heady *brew* was cooking in this "quiet" town. Something a hell of a lot more important than an island hardsite. Hardsites were never *causes*—they were effects. And *something* was brewing that would demand a hardsite—a fantastic damn hardsite—for back-up.

Cosa di tutti Cosi, sure—but how, what? What was the *angle?*

For the first time since L.A., Bolan felt *behind* the problem.

L.A. had been a disaster.

Seattle would be, too, unless Bolan could get *out*

97

front—and damned quick. His combat guts were telling him so. When they talked, Bolan listened. And, at the moment, they were speaking in many tongues.

They, too, were *brewing*.

At least, now, he had a line on the next domino.

Wooded area, right. Narrow winding trails for roads, hills and dales, trees and water, wildlife. Paradise. A misty night without moon or stars, a chill in the air that soaked to the bone, utter pitch blackness that could give a guy vertigo if he didn't have some reference to reality.

Not paradise, no, not this way.

Bolan's reference was his own feet in wet grass, the chirrup of tree-dwelling insects, a sense of oneness with the night.

Sure, the night was his brother. Bolan should have been an Indian—several hundred years ago. He would lay in tall grass and wait for his brother, the bear, to hit the trail for food or water—then Bolan the Bold would rise up, bone knife in hand, to stalk and liberate the holy spirit from his brother and apologize for returning it to the universe unfulfilled. From that victory would come food for the tribe, a warm robe for the night chill, bones for tools and more weapons—a victory dance with honors from the old men.

But Bolan the Bold was not an Indian.

He did not lay in wait for his brother, the bear.

His kill would bring no profit his tribe would applaud, his victory no honors.

He was a soldier without convention; he stalked his brother, rapacious man; his final victory would be his ultimate defeat; he would be buried in dishonor.

That was reality, and that was another sort of reference.

He'd left his vehicle far to the rear, responding to a sense of caution born long ago and reinforced on a Seattle waterfront less than twenty-four hours earlier.

Whatever the game, it was being played for high stakes.

He accepted the stakes, not even knowing what they were, and played the game by that sense of value. He would not be trapped by a layered defense this time.

And he was not.

The unmistakable burping chatter of Thompsons in fast unload came from three hundred yards in, two at once in sustained bursts that shattered the calm of the night and slew paradise for certain. The muted glow from the cabin up there was still no more than an indistinct shimmering of the mists.

Bolan had not even come close. And as he circled warily toward the road, armed with only the 9mm Beretta and stalking now only the uncertainties of the night, he saw the flare-up of automobile head-lamps and heard the whine of the vehicle as it spun out of the graveled drive, the screech of tires finding purchase on asphalt pavement.

A lot of things came together in the combat mind during that infinitesimal moment of decision. Then he was crashing through the underbrush in a dead run through blackest night, on an intersecting course and damning himself for failing to awaken to truth five minutes earlier.

He got there several heartbeats ahead of the fleeing headlamps and fired on the run, dispatching a full clip without breaking stride—then diving and reloading as the shattered vehicle swerved abruptly and headed across the road to the woods on the opposite side.

It smacked head-on into a tree, veered off and swung around to break itself open upon another.

Yeah—his brother, the car.

Flames erupted immediately, spreading quickly and flashing up to engulf the wreckage in an all-consuming bonfire.

Bolan found an ejected body ten feet from the flaming pyre, entirely dead and minus a foot. It was a familiar body. He'd soft-touched it on an ambitious island some sixteen hours ago.

Stay soft, he muttered, and continued the evaluation.

There was no saying for sure, but what evidence lay quickly available disclosed a hit crew of but three men. A small crew, and Bolan was certain this time there were no layers. An easy hit. Sure.

He ran on up the road and into the cabin.

It was nice. Bolan himself would enjoy this cabin. One big room, with a loft. Fireplace across one wall, small kitchen and dining area, the rest living space in knotty pine and open-beam ceiling, casual furniture scattered about.

Two big logs danced flames in the fireplace. Spread in front of that cheery scene was a thick white rug of soft, nubby material. It would never be pure white again. Sprawled upon it in grotesque attitudes of violent death were the naked bodies of a man and a woman.

He was, sure, Allan Nyeburg.

She was some pretty young loser who'd found the easy way the hardest. Pretty, once. Now she and her partner in death were virtually chewed to hamburger by an untold quantity of big mean .45 caliber dum-dums.

Bolan reached between them to pick up a bloody marksman's medal. Cute. But no thanks. The Executioner would not take credit for this one, not this way.

Easy hit, yeah.

And you really blew it—didn't you, Allan? You had it all going for you, guy. Had it all. Brains, education, looks, charm—even a halfway decent business base to build upon. Then a real cool lady and a daughter any man would claim—and you blew it, guy, *you blew it!* For what?

Bolan's gaze traveled along that misused young female body punched out there, and he wondered if Nyeburg had actually *seen* any of them.

His brother, the satyr.

Bolan had known alkies and junkies, compulsive gamblers and suicidals of very persuasion—but this was the first guy he'd ever known to actually screw himself into the grave.

He shook his head and went away from there.

Scratch another domino. Sorry, Margaret, but that's all the guy had ever been. A domino. With no chain —no chain at all.

And what a hell of a brew it was getting to be.

As he withdrew to his vehicle, Bolan found his thoughts centering around Margaret Nyeburg. Why Margaret? Why not the junior edition, with whom he'd shared so much of mind and flesh?

They were a contrast, those two—so alike yet so different— so *together* yet so apart. It was no simple matter of generation gap. There was something basically offkey.

His mind could not touch it.

Only his guts could.

He needed a talk with Margaret. Suddenly, almost

desperately, that demand rose up from the animal side of his consciousness.

So okay. He would go for a parley with the cool lady.

11: SCORCHED

He left the car at the end of the lane and continued on by foot. The mists were in full sway once again at waterside—now concealing, now revealing with a ragged bottom edge that seemed to raise and lower in unpredictable patterns. The lights from the beach house were dim, barely visible through the shifting fog but still a beacon in the gloom drawing Bolan inexorably toward some deepfelt if intellectually unrecognizable crisis—like a moth, he supposed, homing on a candle's flame, compelled by some universal force beyond comprehension to seek its own certain destruction.

Bolan recognized the feeling, and it was the reaction thereto that dictated the wary approach. With a momentary flashback of consciousness, he was in enemy country again and that was a VC hut perched at the edge of a ricefield. There was no way to know what awaited him there, but he did know that a pursuing enemy band were sniffing along his trail and already combing through the rice paddy at his rear. Certain death lay behind, an uncertain goal ahead. The hut could mean brief sanctuary or imprisonment, solace or pain, survival or extinction—but it was beckoning him and he went, all the while aware of the moth and the flame.

Of such incomprehensible directions are the destinies of men written and fulfilled, especially Mack Bolan's sort of man.

The "rear base" beach house was a simple, oblong structure with a single bedroom, bath, a larger area without walls that served for cooking, dining, lounging—small porch to the rear, a screened porch on the beach side.

He circled the building once, picking up no vibrations of life within or without, then went to the rear and quietly let himself in. Two small table lamps were softly lighting the living area. The door to the bedroom was closed. Diffused light spilled from the open bathroom doorway to illuminate the closet-size hallway separating bedroom and bath.

There was not a sound upon the place.

The night was young but the women could have turned in early—it had been a traumatic day for both.

That uneasy feeling was still ruling Bolan's guts, though; he moved softly along the wall of the large room and sprang the Beretta.

Margaret picked that moment to walk out of the bathroom, wearing absolutely nothing but a small towel wound about the head like a turban.

She spotted Bolan immediately and froze in mid-stride with a soft exclamation of dismay.

It was a body to make young men wish they were older and old men yearn for youth one more time around, glowing with the soft allure of mellowed maturity yet youthful in carriage and striking of form.

And Bolan knew, in a flash of understanding, at least part of the answer to the contrasts between mother and daughter. Dianna was a beautiful kid, sure—all fresh and sparkling and natural—but Bolan now understood that *natural* could also mean *raw*.

That lady standing there, for all her naked embarassment, was a rare piece of feminine art—refined and polished and fully turned beyond the *raw* by the craftswoman who lived within.

He told her, "Dammit, Margaret, I won't apologize for staring."

She replied, with a cool blend of embarassment and humor, "I should hope not," and disappeared back the way she'd come.

The experience had been hardly more than a flash —but it was a flash that illumined. Bolan would not soon forget.

She reappeared a moment later with a large bath-towel securely in place, cinched in at the armpits and covering to about midthigh. With a nervous laugh, she confessed, "You scared another strand of gray into my hair."

Bolan apologized for that and waved away her own quiet explanation for nudity. He had not, after all, prepared the ladies for an overnight visit away from home.

He guided her to a chair at the small dining table and sat her down, then pulled a chair for himself close alongside and told her, "I have grim news."

"I'm prepared for it," she replied, looking away, though.

"Allan is dead."

"I see."

"Not by my hand. Someone beat me to him. He was silenced."

Her eyes were moist when they returned to his gaze. "That's twice," she said simply, in a voice that nearly broke.

Bolan understood. Twice a widow. "Sorry," he muttered.

"Where is he?"

"Cabin, Sammamish area. Know it?"

She shook her head. "Allan had several secret places. How did he die?"

"Quickly."

She understood. "Do you have a cigarette, Mr. Bolan?"

He lit one and placed it at her hand. "I've never lived in your moccasins, Margaret," he said quietly. "If you want to scream and yell, go ahead."

She gave him a half-bright smile and took a pull at the cigarette. "The time for screaming and yelling is long past," she replied. "I had already decided to divorce Allan. Awaiting only the right moment. There's been so much . . . *intrigue* of late. Still . . . well, there is an ache. I can't help that."

"Wouldn't want you to," he commented gruffly. "Can we talk a little?"

"Of course."

"How long had Allan been in this thing? To your knowledge?"

"I suppose . . . about a year. It began with a business trip to New York. Suddenly Allan became involved in real estate, proxy purchases. Then the Expo thing, shipping, meetings with strange men. Life didn't become frantic until just the past month or so, though. Since then it has been mysterious telephone conversations at all hours, armed men lurking about—that pathetic child, Tommy Rentino, forever in Allan's shadow. Was he a bodyguard?"

Bolan shrugged. "If so, nobody figured your husband for being in much jeopardy. Tommy is not a very hard man."

The lady sighed. "Poor Tommy. He was madly in love with Dianna. A hopeless, hurting sort of crush, you know." The eyes flashed at Bolan. "Dianna favors more mature men."

"How *is* Dianna? She had a rough—"

"I sent her away."

Bolan stared at the lady, thoughts chugging and images frozen. "You did what?"

"She has conflicting loyalties, Mr. Bolan. I convinced her that she should make a decision and act accordingly."

He growled, "I need more than that, Margaret."

"She has a lover," the lady reported, sighing.

So what and why not? As the young lady herself had observed, it wasn't 1940—and, even then, many young ladies had lovers. But why had Boland blithely overlooked even the question?

He told the young lady's mother, "I still don't understand. Unless you're saying that I'm a threat to her morals. There's a much larger threat waiting out there for your daughter, and it—"

She halted his speech with a pained expression and a hand at his shoulder. "No, not that. I said 'conflict' and that is exactly what I meant. Dy paced around here for an hour, crying and wringing her hands. She's not nearly so sophisticated as she appears, Mr. Bolan. Dy is a—well, a very direct sort. She handles emotions at the heart level. She—"

"What's the conflict?"

"You. And John Franciscus."

"Who's he?"

The lady shook her head. "Dy met him through some association with Allan. I hadn't heard of *them*, though, until just today. Until Dy began pacing and crying, in fact. But I gather that he is in the enemy camp."

It was a nutty family, Bolan was deciding. The lady had sent the Executioner after her husband, presumably because the man was a detestable criminal type whom she could simply not condone—married to it or not. The lady's daughter, who supposedly hated her stepfather, made love to his executioner and pleaded for his life though marked for death, herself, by the guy's associates. Now the mother was telling the executioner that she'd "sent" her daughter into the death camp because of "conflicting" loyalties—an affair of the heart with one of the enemy.

Bolan shook his head to clear it and growled, "Wait a minute, now."

"She felt that she had to at least try."

"Try what?"

"Stop the killing."

"And how would she go about doing that?"

"I haven't the faintest idea. But she felt compelled to try."

"You're lying to me, Margaret," Bolan decided. "You didn't advise Dianna to do anything of the sort. You didn't 'send' her anywhere."

The gaze wavered and broke. The lady sighed. She said, "I suppose I'm not a very good liar. You're right, of course. I tried every piece of logic at my command—but Dy makes her own decisions, ill-based though they may often be." The artful version of Dianna Webb raised creamy shoulders slightly and dropped them. "She left here barely an hour behind you. I promised her that I would remain at least until morning, in case you should return."

"She didn't expect me to return, did she?"

Margaret's gaze returned level to his. "No."

"She was going to turn me over."

"I believe that was the general intent."

"How was she going to do that?"

"Don't blame her too strongly, Mr. Bolan. She is quite young. And confused about love."

Bolan said, "Yeah. How?"

108

"She had a rather detailed description of your—your motor home."

A moth to the candle, yeah. Bolan got up quickly and killed the lights in the living area. "Get dressed!" he commanded.

"I don't understand."

"Don't even try. Just do as I say. I'm taking your life back into *my* hands, Margaret. Now come on! Do you go dressed or do you go like that?"

"I'll dress," she whispered.

Bolan's guts were now yelling in forty forked tongues. He growled, "Second thought, forget it!" He grabbed her by the arm and hustled her to the screen porch, then pushed her low and led her through the doorway, taking her by the hand there and urgently whispering, *"Run!"*

They broke cover at the front corner and plunged blindly into the mists toward the water on a dead run, and they had not covered twenty yards when the chilling staccato of choppers in concert tore the silence behind them.

Margaret faltered and almost fell. Bolan jerked her on and put an arm about her to keep her moving.

Three and possibly four Thompsons were taking that house apart at close range—and the lady understood the implications of that as well as Bolan did.

"Oh Dy, Dy!" she moaned.

"She couldn't have known," Bolan assured her.

They were circling toward the drive when flames shot skyward back there along the water and a rumbling explosion shook the ground beneath their feet.

The death crew had come to "stop the killing." Apparently they'd known that Bolan was in there, and they were leaving no stone unturned nor board unburnt.

Scorched earth, sure.

A lone gunner had been posted at Bolan's rented Fairlane. He took the guy from behind, with a garrote —and the moth and the lady shook the flames of that place from their wings.

Close, yeah. Too damned close for chuckles.

12: VALUABLES

Leo Turrin sent his tagman on with the rest of the crew to handle the formalities of registration while he stopped off at the message desk.

But there were no messages for "Joe Petrillo."

He proceeded on to a telephone booth at the far side of the lobby and made a coin call to his unlisted "cold drop" in Pittsfield, an automated answering system.

The connection was made and he fed in the verbal coder which would trigger the electronic brain to a release of messages stored since the last check-in.

There was but one, very brief—but the one which Turrin had been anxiously awaiting all day.

"This is Striker," announced a familiar voice. "Tap me at the floater, Seattle, two thousand and two hundred."

That was it, but it was plenty.

Turrin hung up and gazed at his watch. Twenty-two hundred meant ten o'clock. What the guy really meant, though, was ten minutes *past* that hour. He would answer *no* ring except at that precise moment.

"Floater" was, of course, the mobile number in the guy's vehicle.

You didn't simply pick up a phone and call Mack Bolan—not even if you happened to be the guy's only contact with the straight world. You called at

111

ten past ten, if that's what the man wanted, then you called every hour after that until you connected.

It was now nine fifty, Seattle time.

Turrin went into the smoke shop and bought some cigars, then returned to the lobby in time to intercept the dumb but loyal tagman, Jocko Frensi.

"Go on up with the stuff," Turrin instructed him. "I'm going to hang around and make a few calls without switchboards. What's our room?"

"Ten hundred," Fresni reported with a woebegone frown. "Man says it's the best in the joint, but I dunno, it's only got one teevee. Uh, don't you think I better stay down here with you?"

"Naw, it's okay. Go on. You look beat. Boys on the same floor?"

"Yeh. We can open the doors and connect with them if we wanta. Pers'nally, boss, I don't wanta."

Fresni had once ridden some of the best mounts in thoroughbred racing circles. That was years ago. The little guy's last horse died under him, literally, and Jocko damn near died with him. He'd never been right in the head, since. Fast man with a blaster, though, and as loyal a bodyguard as would be found anywhere. And he really did look beat.

Turrin stepped over to his chief torpedo and told him, "See that Jocko goes right to bed. You guys leave 'im alone. Stay in your own damn rooms."

"Yeh, sure," the guy growled back. "We're going to get some broads, anyway. What're you going to be doing?"

"Nosing around. Stay close to the rooms."

"You want a broad?"

Turrin seemed to be considering the idea before he replied, "Guess not. What do they call that—jet lag? Hell it's about one o'clock back home."

112

The head cock laughed and said, "You're getting old, Leo."

Turrin allowed that kind of familiarity. Many bosses didn't. But Leo had a loyal crew. They knew what they could and couldn't—there was no need for squeezing their tails in the bargain.

He chuckled and tipped the bellman in advance then watched men and luggage into the elevator before turning away and looking for somewhere to kill another fifteen minutes.

His wandering took him outside to sample the air. The damn town was pregnant. It was about to give birth to something, that was sure. That atmosphere was loaded with something more than moisture.

He went back inside—located the bar, the coffee shop, barbers, main dining room—then found his way back to the pay telephones at precisely ten-oh-nine.

He dialed the mobile operator, gave her the number, and sat back with an eye to the sweep second hand of his watch.

Bingo—he got the connection at precisely ten-ten.

"Yeh, who'd you want?"

"Guy name Striker, also known as Tony." Which meant there was no gun at Leo Turrin's head.

"That was quick," Bolan's normal voice replied. "I just filed the request thirty minutes ago and hauled down for a long wait."

"Got it twenty minutes ago. I'm in town. What's on?"

"Damned if I know," the big one replied soberly. "I was hoping you could tell me."

"All I know is, for sure, about two hundred descending for head. You got a spare one?"

Bolan chuckled, but it was a dry sound—like steel on steel. "Not lately. Two hundred, eh? Heavy?"

113

"You'd better believe heavy. Best in the west. What the hell're you up to?"

"I think we'd better meet. I don't like these mobiles."

"Know what you mean. Okay. When and where?"

"How flexible are you?"

"Not very. I'm in party. But you name it, I'll be there. Somehow."

"Okay, let's give it a couple of hours. Make it three. Pick you up at the science fair building, by the fountains. Say one o'clock."

"Okay. Uh, Bigpush may want to come along. Okay?"

The Bolan voice flattened somewhat as he inquired, "He here, too?"

"Supposed to be. We haven't connected yet but probably will before one."

"What'd he bring?"

"Fifty. Maybe another fifty, shortly."

"Come to play, or to watch?"

"To play, I think. With a big worry."

"Okay. Bring him if it's his idea."

"Gotcha. Say, man. Stay hard."

"You too."

Turrin patted the telephone and hung it up, then crossed the lobby to the message desk for another check-in.

And, yeah—it was there that time, Brognola's side of the equation.

He strolled back to the phone booths, casually tossing a dime and reflecting on the crazy life he led.

At the edge of a knife, sure—balanced precariously between two worlds, and none whatever for himself.

So why'd he do it?

Why did singers sing and dancers dance? Leo Turrin was no philosopher.

A guy simply did what he did best.

Bolan turned away from the mobile phone and lay a friendly gaze on his guest of necessity, Margaret Nyeburg. "Feeling better?" he asked, unnecessarily. It was quite obvious that she was.

The lady was perched atop his plotting table in the war room, fresh from a renewing if brief shower —legs crossed and feet drawn up under her, dwarfed and childlike in Bolan's dungaree jacket which was the only thing between them at the moment. Lovely, vulnerable, strongly appealing. Bolan found himself regretting even more strongly than ever his earlier involvement with the daughter. Some things just wouldn't work. A mother-daughter situation was one of those things.

A mug of scalding coffee was cooling precariously between her thighs. Bolan moved it, noting her silence, and said, "I guess you are. Feeling better. Eh?"

She sniffed and said, "I just hope I haven't caught a nasty cold. You're a strong young man, Mack. Thank you. That's silly, isn't it? How can I thank you?"

He'd caught that "young man" coder, and understood. She was telling him to keep away. He intended to.

He told her, "We're alive. That's thanks enough."

"For you, good. For me—well, it seems the least of consolations."

He growled, "Hey, hey."

"I can't help it. It's just all so miserable, so impossible."

He said, for about the tenth time, "Margaret—

115

Dianna did not know what she was getting you into. Believe that."

"I guess you're right," she said, sighing. "I have to believe it, don't I? Dy is all I have in the world."

His gaze shifted. "That's very sad."

"Is it? Why? Some people don't have that much."

"You're what?—thirty-eight?—forty?"

She wrinkled her nose and replied, "Squarely between those two. Diplomacy isn't one of your strong points, is it?"

"Not usually. At the age of thirty-nine, Margaret, all you have of value to your life is a daughter?"

She fidgeted under that penetrating scrutiny. "Well . . . okay. I was being dramatic. No, dammit, I wasn't. What else *do* I have to brag about? Why not be honest with one's self? What *do* I have, Mack?"

He raised a hand and ticked off the points on his fingers as he called to her attention, "Frustration, self-pity, lack of direction, isolation, death instinct. That's five negatives." He raised the other hand. "Now you count me off five positives to balance that —and I'll *tell* you what you've got, lady."

"You're doing fine," she replied in a muffled voice, obviously offended by his tone. "Keep counting."

"Okay. You've got beauty, brains, heart, ethics, and a desire to be happy. I could probably count twenty more positives. You want to know what you've got? You've got the world by the very *ass*, lovely lady."

She flinched. "That's what I said, you're no diplomat."

"And you're no valid object of pity," he growled.

"What was it Dy called you? A *tough* guy? You are! Tough as an angry old bull, aren't you! And you expect everyone else to be just as tough!"

"That's right," he said softly. "I do. When it comes to standing up and proclaiming life, I sure do."

"You're preparing me for something," she decided, eyes flaring. "What is it?"

"Don't base it all on your daughter," he muttered. "That's all I'm getting at. Life goes on, Margaret. Base it on yourself, and what you can do with it."

Fear began at the eyes and radiated to the entire face. "What are you saying? Is Dianna . . . ?"

He turned away from that naked terror. No, he was no damned diplomat—nor was he a dreamer. He'd been there, many times, at the finish of too many Diannas—and, sure, he knew the realities. And he'd decided long ago that there were those times when deception and half-truths in the name of mercy were more painful in the long run than squarely facing the truth.

He told Dianna's mother, "I couldn't get longshot odds from even a guy like Jimmy the Greek on that girl's chances, Margaret."

"But surely . . ."

"Here's a surely," he said coldly. "She's playing with brutes, she'll be brutalized."

"*John* is not a brute! *John* is a . . . !" Those eyes flared again, fizzled, fell, and she finished with a whispered, "Oh well."

"John, huh. Nice guy, huh. Okay, Margaret, you tell me all about nice guy John. This time you hold back nothing. Hear me? Nothing! This is no cute parlor game, dammit. Your daughter's life is hanging over the edge. You *saw* how those guys operate! I've seen a lifetime of it! Now dammit, give me the key! Give it to me! Give me the damned key, Margaret!"

"You'd still help her? After all . . . ?"

117

"Oh for God's crying children! What the hell *am* I? We're talking about a *kid! Your* kid!"

"All right!" The lady was weeping. "I'll tell you. I'll give you your damned key!"

In the back of his brain, Bolan knew that an important domino had just toppled.

Up front, however, that was the least consideration.

More than dominoes, right now, he wanted Dianna Webb—alive and whole. Even if he had to drag her out of there screaming and kicking.

13: HOPE

Seattle was a town that had seen its highs and lows
—and was right now sitting somewhere in the middle, but with great hopes.

Beginning as a small lumber settlement in mid-
nineteenth century and named after a local Indian
chief, it received first substantial growth with the
coming of the railroad in post-Civil War days then
boomed into the turn of the century via the Alaskan
gold rush, serving as chief port of supply and support
during those fevered times, establishing itself as a
major seaport for all times.

Growth had been mostly upward throughout the
twentieth century, except for a few bad moments
from time to time. Principal city of the Pacific Northwest, she'd surged mightily during W.W. II as a
major shipping and shipbuilding center, then gone into the expansive semi-peacetime era as the seat of
a growing military-industrial complex—with emphasis on aerospace and related technological sophistries.

Recent problems in the American aerospace in-
dustry had been particularly hard felt in Seattle—
where a single large company had employed more
than 100,000 skilled and professional workers only to
drop its payroll to a lean force of 30,000 during a
slump that still was evident. Dependent segments
of the local economy were as badly hit, and the en-

tire area was impacted by this mini-depression.

It was a town with guts, though, and a brave past. There were few outward signs of a city in trouble. She wore a happy face even if the guts were strained a bit—and Bolan liked the town. The beauty of the natural setting was unequalled anywhere. Built on seven hills and containing within her own boundaries four lakes and forty-five parks, majestically flanked by the Cascades east and the Olympics west—this beautiful city on Puget Sound held something worthwhile for any taste and every pursuit.

And that, at the moment, was what worried Mack Bolan.

In times of strain, overanxious city fathers would be more inclined to support rather than spurn new hope in the economic sector. They would, perhaps, rush to embrace without first closely scrutinizing.

And, yes, based on the meager revelations of Margaret Nyeburg alone, this appeared to be precisely the case at hand.

John Franciscus was a man with "an open past" but a peculiarly clouded present. If Nyeburg had been the *face* of the mob encroachment here, then Franciscus was most probably the *muscle*.

And that was a bit difficult to square with the known record. The guy was about Bolan's age. Like Bolan, he'd spent most of his adult life in the military —but with a difference. Franciscus was a West Pointer. He'd been a combat soldier, not a politician. Yet he seemed to have many political and social contacts, plenty of money, seemingly unlimited resources. He did not work, had not been born wealthy, and was not visibly attached to any business or financial concerns.

Margaret referred to him as "that playboy."

Allan, though, had been "frightened" by him, Dianna "clearly imbalanced" by him, and certain civic officials seemingly over-responsive to his "promotions."

Why that last? What was the guy offering Seattle that she did not already possess? Margaret could not answer that. Bolan thought that perhaps he could —with just a few more pieces of the puzzle in place.

The mission of the moment, however, was not to drain Johnny Franciscus but to spring Dianna Webb. Bolan had not been playing games with Margaret Nyeburg. He felt most overpoweringly that the lady's daughter was another moth with fragile wings fluttering too close to the consuming flame.

Bolan knew his enemy.

He knew their values, the things they revered, the prices they were willing to pay for success. And they would pay any *life* but their own.

If not already too late, he meant to see that Dianna Webb did not become part of that price.

Bolan checked the lady into a Holiday Inn under an assumed name, paid for the room cash in advance, and spirited her into the room wrapped in a blanket —with promises that she would remain until contacted and "play no more games."

Then he went to work on the warwagon, changing a few color panels to present a new "design"—replacing the license plates—rearranging various exterior dummy appurtenances.

The hour was nearing eleven when he wheeled the sleek "new" motor home to an address in Seattle's east-central sector. It was a high-rise complex in a parklike setting overlooking Lake Washington—an elite neighborhood for fashionable cavedwellers— security conscious, with electronic door interlocks at each building entrance, uniformed patrols on the grounds between the buildings and in the parking areas.

One building in particular did not seem overly confident of the normal security precautions. It was the address in Bolan's warbook. A car was parked at the yellow zone curbing just down from the lobby entrance, two guys in the front seat. Four more guys in well-fitted suits stood in a clutch at the entrance, chatting.

Not the usual mob guys, no. Soldiers nonetheless. Each of those four would have looked more natural in shiny combat boots and the spiffy trappings of the Military Police. That was Bolan's gut reading, at any rate.

He donned the yellow nightshades, pulled on to the curb directly opposite the entrance, and opened his window.

It was as good a time as any to probe the depths of Dianna Webb's defection.

Four pairs of eyes took that vehicle instantly apart, but none of the troops moved another muscle.

Bolan called over, "Pardon me. Which building is forty-two?"

One of the guys peeled away from the pack to take a couple of paces toward the curb. "This is forty," he replied in a not unfriendly tone. "Go back around the circle and take the first right. That should put you into forty-two."

Bolan said, "Thanks," as another of the four moved forward and squatted to peer at his undersides.

"That's quite an RV," the new one commented, coming out of the squat to flash a grin at the man at the wheel. "How's she do in the mountains?"

"I'll find out tomorrow," Bolan replied, grinning back. "Taking her up Olympus."

122

"I'd be interested in how she does," the guy shot back. "You live around here?"

"Not yet. Buddy of mine lives over in forty-two. We're spending the night here, taking off early tomorrow morning."

"What's his name?"

"Thompson. Know 'im?"

"Wish I did, no."

"Come in and take a look around if you'd like," Bolan grandly offered.

Genuine regret registered there as the guy flashed a sheepish glance toward his companions. "Some other time, I'd love to. How much it set you back?"

"God I hate to look at the papers and see," Bolan said, grinning. "It started out at thirty, basic. I just closed my eyes and signed my name. I'll look at the final price after I see how she does."

The guy laughed and stepped back. "I'll look you up when you get back."

"Do that," Bolan said, and moved on away from there.

No—not standard mob guys. These "boys" were all business—in a polished military manner. A high percentage of that friendly banter had been business-oriented. The guy dug the rig, sure—but he'd been primarily interested in establishing the status of it. Apparently Bolan had passed the inspection. Just as apparently, Dianna had betrayed his confidence.

He circled on to the next building and into the parking area separating the two, found a good spot for surveillance, and parked.

Thirty thousand, hell. Start at a hundred thousand, soldier, and work up from there. She quietly boasted the most sophisticated of electronic and optic systems developed during the space age; no expense had been spared toward that consideration.

She could "see" for more than a mile with telescopic/stereoscopic clarity, night or day, and she could "hear" flies buzzing at two thousand yards—unaided by any exterior devices. With exterior implantations in the target area, the bonus baby to Bolan's war effort could scan through walls of buildings and record conversations in a dozen simultaneous operations. And that was far from all.

But it was all the use Bolan had in mind for the present, and it was time for the battle cruiser to go to work.

He went to the console and activated the audio surveillance system, directing the concealed barrel pickups to a point near the very peak of 40 Washington Towers, then turned on the "nitebrite optics," an infra-red system coupled with laser techniques for pencil-flash or broadflood selectivity.

Minutes later, he had a rather valid understanding of the problem confronting him.

The Franciscus apartment was the penthouse suite —the only dwelling at that level. There were no exterior approaches. Through a crack in a small half-window—probably a bathroom—he'd picked up the muffled sounds of a television program mixed with occasional bumps, movements, and footfalls somewhere within—a couple of "live" male voices and two audible words: "Johnny said."

He worked up a graphic projection of the building on the plotting board and experimented with several "breach plans" before finally going to the mobile phone and calling his friend the mob flyboy, Jack Grimaldi.

The guy must have been sitting on the telephone. He answered at the first crack of the bell with a breathless, "Yeah, Terrifying Flying Service."

Bolan chuckled and said, "Jack, how soon can you lay hands on a windmill?"

"Had one standing by all day. Thought you'd never call. What's the job?"

"Remember Dallas?"

"Oh God. That again. That was daylight, buddy."

"So you try a little harder this time," Bolan suggested. "It's only about four hundred feet, though, Jack. Will the weather allow?"

"Depends on where you are. Over on the coast it's zero-zero right now. Mountains have most of it blocked but it's seeping down Juan de Fuca and spilling down along the Sound. If you're—"

"Western shore of Lake Washington, Jack."

"That's different. Just a minute."

Grimaldi was "gone" for a full minute. Bolan marked time by studying his projections. The pilot returned to say, "Okay, it looks hopeful if we move right quick. You've got a ground layer of thin stuff with tops at about two hundred feet. The Naval Air Station over there at Sand Point says it's acceptable but subject to change very rapidly. Then there's another deck at one thousand and already descending. There's no way to know how long it will take to close solid—you know what I'm saying? We could have a zero-zero condition over there from a thousand feet on down if those two layers decide to marry."

"We'll have to risk it, Jack. Let's at least go up and eyeball it from the top."

"Right. Where do I get you?"

"Come down to the Union Bay bridge. Then keep south and put on your infra-red specs. Look for a beacon. I'll be at the bottom."

"What if I can't see the damn beacon?"

125

"It's laser-focused. You'll see it. Just in case, though—give me a comm channel."

"Okay," the pilot soberly replied, "let's see . . . how about 126.7 megs? You have that?"

"I can plug it in, yeah. That's a standard aero freq, isn't it?"

"Well sure. That's all these buggies come with. Just watch what you say. You're Low Boy. I'm High Boy."

"Right. Radio silence, though, unless you get lost."

"Right."

"How soon, Jack?"

"Let's see . . . what will I need?"

"Guts and skill."

Grimaldi chuckled. "What else? Give me something I can handle."

"Better have a rope ladder, Jack. I guess that's about the only special. Oh, no . . . if you have a basket . . ."

The pilot groaned. "You going after a basket case?"

"Could be. Better be ready for it."

"Okay. Give me five minutes to prep, another five to fly. See you in ten. I hope."

Yeah, sure, *hope*.

There was damn little else to cling to.

14: NUMBERED

The tall buildings rose eerily from the low-level mists, stark in their isolation, foreboding, capped with twinkling red lights as a warning to low-flying aircraft—a hazard, yeah, one hell of a fine hazard.

Bolan pushed a sketch onto the pilot's knee-clip and circled a spot with his finger. "This one, the two o'clock position, Jack. Let's take a low pass for looksee. Tell me if you can put down there."

Grimaldi whistled softly into his headset. "If we can't, Sarge, I'd recommend a scrub. We've only got about four hundred feet to play with, and it's closing fast. If we're down when it closes, well, okay. We can always lift off and pray for someplace to land. *You* get down there, though, and the clouds settle around those damned windows—well, enough said. I couldn't get back for you."

Bolan growled, "Yeah. Go look."

They went by in a slow pass, circling at fifty feet above. The roof was a jumble of utility structures, air-conditioners, supports for the hazard-lighting tower—bounding it all in, a steel parapet about four feet high.

Grimaldi was the first to note the clear area. "Southeast corner," he said, elated. "There's room."

Bolan's attention had been diverted elsewhere. Two men, in foul-weather hoods, were huddled

127

against a small housing near the north parapet. And they had spotted the chopper immediately, were watching it with considerable interest.

"Go around again, Jack. Couple of bandits at twelve o'clock."

"Where?"

"Small structure at the north wall. Elevator, maybe —or stairwell. Let's make them nervous."

The pilot grinned and kicked the little ship into a steep descent, crabbing around in a near-spin to skim dangerously along the rooftop.

Both men ran into the open, electrified by the stunt and obviously shaken.

Bolan was threading the sound-suppressor aboard the Beretta. He was rigged for light combat—black-suit, AutoMag, Beretta, chest pouch, single utility belt.

"Give me a razzle-dazzle approach," he instructed the pilot. "Go in like an eagle. I'll clear the area and keep going. Lift off in three minutes, that's three exactly, with or without me. If it's without, stand by upstairs for another five—if you can—but that's my point of no return. Take off and don't look back."

"Gotcha," Grimaldi replied. "Like an eagle, huh? How's this?"

The little bird went into a steep climb then heeled, tilted, and swooped back across the rooftop with hairbreadth clearance. The guys below were running for the open area and waving hardware, now, but they hit the deck and hugged it as the "eagle" swooped overhead.

Grimaldi was a master at his work. Forward motion halted with a quick upward jerk, followed immediately by a quick drop and a hover with the skids probably no more than six inches above the deck.

Bolan hit the hatch with a "Tally-ho!" at his lips

128

and the whispering Beretta streaking flame from his right hand.

The two "bandits" were caught midway in a scramble for footing, and never quite made it. Bolan paused above them for a moment to verify the results then jogged on to the housing where their presence had first been noted.

And, yeah, it was an elevator. Limited duty, two stops only, the penthouse and the floor below it. Perfect.

He called the car and stepped quickly inside, punched the penthouse button, and erupted from there at that level with the Beretta Belle in whispering attack.

A guy on a stool at the opposite wall got his mouth open and never found time to close it, a 9mm Parabellum slug zipping in there with shattering impact and splattering the wall behind with more life forces than any man could spare.

Another guy, at the end of the lobby area, managed to get a hand inside his coat—his last bloody inch before doomsday.

Bolan reached back into the elevator car and threw the control to "out of service," then propped the door open with the sentry stool just to make certain. There was no other elevator service to this level. Penthouse visitors evidently were required to transfer cars at the next level down. An emergency stairway with a fire door was the only other access.

He stepped across the guy at the entrance to the apartment and kicked the door open.

An MP type just inside gawked then gurgled under the impact of another snorter. Bolan kept going and found another in the kitchen then another just exiting from a bathroom—and he left them there where he found them.

A large bedroom with two glass walls was empty; another, a mere cubicle with no glass at all, contained a dresser and a bed with a technically nude young lady spread-eagled and bound to the latter by wrists and ankles. A small handtowel was stuffed into her mouth.

The eyes became frantic at the sight of Bolan, and a muffled moan escaped the gag.

He stood over her and carefully removed the towel, then coolly inquired, "Is this some kinky game or is the young lady in trouble?"

It was a cheap shot, sure, but he was as angry as relieved and just couldn't let the opportunity slide.

She wore only the slinky chemise he'd first seen her in, plus bikini briefs. By her struggles or some other force, the dress had become raised in wadded folds to the breastline.

She turned away from the Bolan gaze and closed her eyes.

"Ready to go home, babe?" he asked her in a kindlier tone.

"God, yes," she whispered.

He cut the sashcord from her wrists and lay the stiletto on her bare belly. "Meet me at the elevator," he instructed. "Where's friend John?"

"I-I don't know for sure. And I don't care for sure. He left hours ago. Something about the Seattle-Tacoma Airport."

Bolan snapped, "Hurry!" and jogged out of there.

He scattered micro pickups all over that joint, even in the bathrooms, then made a run for the lobby.

Dianna was waiting for him there, standing astride the overturned stool in the elevator doorway, teeth bared and corners of the mouth pulled back in a horrified grimace as she stared transfixed at the former occupant of that stool.

130

"Know him?" Bolan growled.

"Yes, th-that's David Turner."

"Was," he said, and pushed her gently on into the car then kicked the stool aside.

He'd just cycled the controls for a return to service when Dianna lunged forward with eyes glaring and a gurgling in the throat, terrified gaze leaping beyond Bolan's shoulder to something behind him.

He whirled to see the fire door half-open, a guy pushing through, others close behind on the stairwell.

The guy in front wore crepe-sole canvas shoes and casual slacks, turtleneck jersey, light nylon windbreaker—handsome guy, wavy blond hair concealing the ears and curling to the rear in a mod fashion, facial expression altering rapidly from annoyance to alarm as those gazes clashed. The man directly behind looked like some moviemaker's impression of Aristotle Onassis—a chubby guy done up in swank suit with silk lapels, a boutonniere, smoked glasses, gray Homburg.

All of which was no more than a flashing impression gained via a microsecond of observation while Bolan was already reacting to the situation.

He launched himself in full flight, hitting that door with a double judo kick from six feet out, and it went all the way to full closure with a resounding crack, punching the blond man and entourage into a noisy descent along the stairway.

Dianna was a quick reactor, also. She'd punched the "door close" control and was holding the door open with her hand when Bolan recovered and began scrambling back. "Roof!" he yelled as he dived inside.

He again cycled to "out of service" as they were exiting, then grabbed the girl's hand and led the dash to the waiting 'copter. While she climbed

131

aboard, he stepped over to attach an "exterior device" to the outside railing of the parapet.

"You still had ten seconds," Grimaldi observed drolly as they lifted off.

"Not really," Bolan puffed, but nobody heard him above the clatter of the rotors.

Nor did they need to.

Angry men were erupting from another housing just east of the stalled elevator and swarming across that roof down there.

One of them took a wild shot at the disappearing "eagle," but it was a vain attempt.

They were well clear and climbing into the mists above.

The girl gave him an uncertain visual contact then sighed and snuggled to him.

Grimaldi was making a sign with his headset.

Bolan donned his and asked, "Yeah?"

"Too close for comfort," the pilot commented. "It's zero-zero down there right now. You just made it, buddy. Thank God I was sitting, not hovering upstairs."

Yeah.

That, dear hearts, was what Mack Bolan called "on the numbers." With not a heartbeat to spare.

15: CLEAN

Grimaldi found a momentary clearing and set down a few hundred yards from where Bolan had left the warwagon.

Grim-lipped, he told the Executioner: "Terrified but safe. For now. Here you are, soldier. And the ride was paid in advance."

Bolan gripped his friend's hand in a warm clasp and said, "You're a real artist, Jack. Thanks. I'm releasing you. Need anything?"

The pilot shook his head. "But you do. I'll stick around a while."

Bolan smiled, lightly slapped the guy's hand, and took the young lady out of there.

As soon as they'd stepped inside the warwagon, she sank to the floor with a happy sound and declared, "I never want to leave here again."

He said, "Come forward," and went up to fire the engine. The girl slid into the seat next to him, contrite but eyes glowing—and he quit that place, headed for the motel where he had parked Margaret.

"Okay," Dianna said presently. "Start screaming at me."

He shot her a stern glance then grinned solemnly as he replied, "Well, we live and learn, don't we. *If* we live."

"That's all? You're not going to slap me around or anything?"

"Do you deserve it?"

"Sure. I guess I cornered all the deserve in town, huh."

"Maybe a pimple of it, here and there. I'm glad you're alive, Dianna. Save the apologies for Margaret. You owe me nothing."

"I owe her, though."

"Yeah."

"I owe you, too. Listen, what can I tell you? What do you need to know?"

He angled another glance her way and shrugged his shoulders. "What do you have?"

"I don't know. Ask me something."

"The blond guy. Was that Franciscus?"

"Yes. The rat. I thought for a little while that you two were very much alike. You're not. Not at all. He almost killed my mother, didn't he."

Bolan nodded. "Trying for me."

Her eyes hung as she reported, "Johnny was furious that they missed. But he didn't bat an eye over the way they handled it—my mother, I mean."

"These people don't care who gets in the way, Dianna."

"Yes, I—you told me that," she pointed out, small voiced. "I had to see it for myself, I guess. I'm sorry, Mack. I am genuinely sorry. For what good that does."

He dismissed it with a bat of the eyes. "Did you see the chubby comic on the stairway behind Franciscus?"

"A while ago?" She slowly shook her head. "It all happened so fast."

"Guy about sixty. Five and a half feet or so high,

134

Big belly, Hollywood glasses. Dressed for burial. Ring any bells?"

She said, "No. I don't recognize that. Maybe it was the important person—yes, I guess it was. They went to the airport to meet someone from Rome."

"Rome, eh?"

"Yes. Someone important. They were all atwitter. That's why I was tied and gagged. They didn't want me to—"

"That's not the only reason," he pointed out.

"I guess not. I tried to get out of there twice to-night, before they tied me up. I guess I was running around and yelling a lot. They were going to kill me, Mack. I know that. Eventually. They were."

He said, "Probably. Homburg from Rome, eh?"

"Huh?"

"Never mind. You keep saying 'they.' Is that a figure of speech, or . . ?"

"No, there's a bunch. Johnny's the boss. They all call him 'Captain' to his face and do everything but salute and kiss his shoes. It made me *sick*. But all those men at the penthouse are sort of like bosses. I mean—well, not David and the ones that just stand around feeling of their guns. But he has about ten other men that come there. Honestly, you know what came in my mind when I was watching them together up there tonight? Hitler and his gang, or something like that. They're all maniacs. But Johnny is the boss maniac. D'you remember me asking you if the little iron cross made you a neo-Nazi? Boy! How close—but the wrong side."

"That's the way they struck you, huh?"

"Sure. Heil Johnny! They do everything but goose-step and wear comic uniforms."

"What do you think they're getting ready for?"

135

"Gosh, I don't know. Except that they're all high, *very* high."

"Okay, let's go back a bit. To Allan. You didn't tell me the whole truth about that, did you?"

Very quietly she replied, "No. I was the first in the family to meet John Franciscus. I went to work for him. Next thing I knew, I was going to bed with him. He was . . ." The girl batted her eyes rapidly and took a deep breath. "I guess I thought he was sent from heaven, gift-wrapped and all. I've noticed that most people get that feeling about him—at first, anyway. He's a rat, though."

"Allan."

"Huh? Oh. Well I was just an avenue to Allan. Not that he had to twist Allan's arm any, but—well, I blame myself for Allan."

"Don't. They knew exactly what they were doing and so did Allan. They hit the guy in his weak spot."

"What?"

"His habit. A very expensive one."

"Yes, I—I guess I hadn't thought of it that way. But that doesn't let me off. I—Mack, I knew what was happening, all along. I mean, generally, though —never any of the particulars. Still don't. But, well, last night, now—when you came storming into that warehouse—well, I simply seized the moment. We thought it was the police. There was no gun at my head."

Bolan solemnly nodded his head at that revelation.

"But I really did pass out. I didn't have to fake that."

"What else did you have to fake?"

"Nothing. I—I wasn't putting you on, Mack. Thor."

He said, "Okay. Things fit better now, anyway. Level with your mother, too, Dianna."

136

She sighed. "I will."

"*Learn* from her. She's got it together pretty well."

"Yes, I guess so. I'll try."

He was wheeling into the *Holiday* parking lot.

"She's in one-oh-four. Her name is Hammond. So is yours, until everything settles around here. Watch yourself, Dy. Take care of it."

"You're not coming in?"

He shook his head. "Things to do. Stay down, this time."

"Will I—will you be coming back?"

"No. This is goodbye. We've seen a lot together. Right? Remember it."

"Oh I will! Kiss me goodbye?"

Their lips met tenderly, briefly.

She said, "You're really something else," and bolted out of there.

He watched her out of sight, then cruised on through and back onto the road, reverse course.

Yes, she was very young. But searching, and growing. That was more than could be said for some.

Bolan heaved a sigh of genuine regret—regret for a lot of things, a lot of people—then he wiped it all clean and cast his mind forward into the night.

There were things to do, yeah. Lots of things.

First, a "collection" pass of 40 Washington Towers. It would be interesting to hear the initial reaction to the strike on the penthouse.

Then that meeting with a real solid guy, Leo Turrin. It wasn't all pain ahead.

137

16: CORPUS DELICTI

Old Hardguts was standing a few feet back off the curb, a solitary figure with coat collar turned up against the mists, snapbrim hat pulled low, unlit cigar clamped between the teeth—breathing through his mouth.

Bolan could have pulled him out of any crowd, at any time. Some undercover guy.

He frowned darkly, recalling that he'd come close to killing the guy once. Not once but several times. That had been *before*, of course. Before Bolan knew who and what Leo Turrin really was. No man in Bolan's memory had earned the respect that this one had. There were few compensations to the life Bolan had chosen; Turrin was one of them.

He pulled to the curb and hit the door control. The center door slid back, and Turrin stepped inside.

"Sarge?"

"Welcome aboard, Leo. Come on up."

"Go around to the other side first. Hal's on the corner next to the building."

Sure, and there was another one. Hal Brognola, super bureaucrat—a man within a man—a public servant who really cared. And, who did not think like a machine, all input/output— he was a cop with soul.

Turrin was marveling at the rig. "You son of a gun! This's some damn rolling palace you've got here!"

Bolan chuckled and replied, "She's got claws, too."

He halted at the opposite corner, door open. Turrin had to call to the guy before he broke cover and hastened aboard.

"What the *hell* is *this*?" Brognola growled.

"Isn't it something?" Turrin said gloatingly, as though it were his own.

"Yeah, it's real peanut butter and bananas," the federal man said sourly. "Stands out like a bawdy house madam in Sunday school. What d'you do with a thing like this?"

"Ask the man who owns one," Turrin replied, wounded.

The two made their way forward and dropped onto the padded side-facing bench opposite the command chair. Bolan grinned and shook steely hands as he eased on past the civic center.

Brognola said, "You're looking well. Better than you have a right to."

"It's the climate," Bolan replied. "Very strong atmosphere out here."

Turrin sniffed and commented, "Say that again. I got about forty pounds of it wedged into my sinuses."

Bolan shot a weighted glance at the man who was perhaps the second or third ranking law enforcement official of the nation. "How're things in paradise, Hal?"

Brognola grinned sourly. "How do you spell that?"

"Try S-H-I-T," said Turrin.

"You ever read that book by Orwell?" Brognola said tiredly. "Well. I can report that Big Brother is alive and well and *running* paradise."

"It's that bad?" Bolan inquired, eyes glinting.

140

"It is."

"Leo was telling me a while back that you're getting kicked upstairs. I guess it hasn't happened yet, eh?"

"Told them I'd resign first," the JD man replied. "But let's talk about *this* Washington. What the *hell* is happening, Striker?"

Bolan smiled to himself. The guy couldn't bring himself to address Bolan by name—probably wouldn't even admit the name to himself, anymore. Sure, it was a tough world, this one. He told the worried friend, "I was hoping you could tell me. The roots are in *your* Washington. This is just the flowering bush, out here. It's some sort of an international deal, Hal. It couldn't work without co-operation from paradise."

"What's involved? Maybe I can add a piece or two if I know the name of the game."

Bolan quickly brought them up to date on the specifics, omitting the Langley Island angle. Then he added, "So this guy Franciscus seems to be the local power center, operating under some franchise from the east."

"We can tell you plenty about that guy," Turrin said. "But it'll keep. Go on, this is getting fascinating."

"Well—the guy is not a made man, I know that. But he's been bringing made VIPs out here for the past three or four months, wining and dining them, taking them on guided tours of some special facility here. And it's *not* the Expo."

"Fair isn't even open yet, is it?" Turrin wondered aloud.

"Soon," Brognola said. "Couldn't there be a connection there?"

"It's possible," Bolan allowed. "It's been a nice

cover so far, for contraband. Could be just as nice a cover for people. But I've found no evidence of direct involvement with the legitimate Expo people."

"Ants at the goddam picnic—to borrow your phrase," Turrin commented. "So where is the picnic? What's big enough in *this* place to warrant all the panic?"

"*Cosa di tutti Cosi,*" Bolan said quietly.

"Sure," Brognola agreed. "That's been a possibility for a long time. But where's the *corpus delicti?*"

"All around you," Bolan muttered. "I'm going to play you a tape that I collected not half an hour ago."

He punched a button on the front panel and swung out a miniature console.

"Hell, would you look at that!" Turrin enthused.

Bolan explained, "I gathered this poop from the Franciscus penthouse. Covers the period from the moment of strike to about forty minutes thereafter. The primary voices you'll hear will be Franciscus and a guy called Helmann. I get this Helmann as a poor man's version of Ari Onassis—considering that anything below that is poor by comparison—a Rebozo, maybe or an Abplanalp. He came here directly from Rome—just arrived tonight—though you'll get the idea from the tape that he's actually based in Zurich."

"I have the picture," Brognola said.

"Run it," said Turrin. "I'm dying from curiosity."

Bolan operated a small electronic keyboard on the console and turned grim concentration to the task of driving the vehicle.

An overhead speaker came alive with the confused sounds of thudding feet, cursing men, doors or something slamming shut.

A loud voice yelled, "That was Bolan, dammit!

142

The son of a bitch, look what he *left* here for God's sake!"

A fainter voice yelled, "He took the chick, Captain!"

"Forget it, forget it! They're not going far! Hey, you people! Help Mr. Helmann there. God I'm sorry about this, Max. What a hell of a way to start! How's that shoulder? Hey! You people round up a heat lamp and get that muscle-mover in here! Mr. Helmann has a very badly bruised shoulder here. God I'm sorry about that, Max. The rotten son of a bitch kicked me right back into you."

"It's all right, Captain," a thickly accented voice assured. "I have survived worse. I shall survive this."

More slamming, shuffling, excited voices overcoming all else. Then a tense announcement, strained, embarrassed: "We lost 'im, Captain."

"You *what?*"

"He had a helicopter on the roof. Got away clean."

A long period of silence preceded the next words, heavily accented speech: "This was one man? He does all this? He kicks Max Helmann downstairs? He shoots up your place and kidnaps a young lady? He drops in by helicopter and as quickly departs, leaving an army of men waving impotently at his departure? This is a safe place for my treasures, Captain?"

Bolan depressed an idler button to explain further. "From here on it jumps back and forth pretty quick, so keep ears alert. My mixer automatically edits time gaps and unintelligible impulses. Thirty recording minutes are compressed into less than ten. Get set, it's heavy stuff."

Leo Turrin actually lit his cigar.

Brognola clamped his jaw and leaned forward, tensely expectant.

143

Bolan released the idler and the sounds returned. He sent the warwagon on a slow cruise along the lakefront, his own shoulders tensed, eyes brooding as he listened for the second time to the clues for the conspiracy of the century.

Ten minutes later, Leo Turrin slumped into his seat with a grim smile. "Well well," he commented drily. "So they're bringing the bucks back home."

Brognola clenched his hands together and growled, "As well as the francs, the marks, the lira, and the pounds. But why here? Why move Switzerland to Seattle?"

"Safer, maybe," Bolan guessed. "It sounds like these guys are preparing for economic doomsday. Maybe they're even manipulating one into existence. A worldwide depression is bound to benefit somebody, isn't it? I'm not much on economics—but in my book, for every loss there's somewhere a gain."

Brognola was frowning, deep in thought. "Me either. Economics, I mean, I don't get. I don't believe the economists understand it, even. But I don't see how the mere location of paper money could mean that much. Do you, Leo?"

"We have a saying in the mob," Turrin replied soberly. "Don't go for the pocket, go for the throat."

"So?"

"They're not talking about paper."

"Langley Island!" Bolan said with a sigh, the light finally dawning.

"Huh?" from Turrin.

Sure. Langley Island. Vaults, not bunkers. Underground vaults in solid rock. Hard storage, sure. A military guard, with heavy firepower and Nazi-like discipline. Bombproof, fireproof, burglar proof. Like Fort Knox.

"Gold," Turrin was saying. "Or silver, maybe. Why

144

not both? I heard just the other day that an old silver quarter is actually worth about two bucks in today's paper. They haven't been minting pure silver for a long time."

Bolan said, "How much of a share would it take, I wonder, to swing the whole world's economy wherever you damn well wanted it?"

"That's a thought," Brognola grimly replied. "I would think, possibly, a very modest share. It works that way with some corporate stocks. You can control with ten to twenty percent."

"What's the latest estimate on worldwide mob worth?" Bolan asked.

"Outta sight!" Brognola replied with a flourish toward the ceiling.

Turrin punctuated that with a quiet, "You know it."

"You guys want to take time for a little jaunt with me?" Bolan asked tautly.

"Where to?"

"Up near Everett, few miles up the coast. A warehouse whose time has come."

"Let me get some marshals on the line," Brognola urged.

"Not yet, Hal. You'd just get your tail kinked. They're strictly legit, so far. I doubt that you could even get a warrant without a lot of hassle through Washington. And, unless I miss my guess, it would be blocked there. I need to expose it first. Then you can move in, and to hell with the warrants. Right?"

"I need to at least get them on standby."

Bolan passed him the mobile phone, and explained, "Big metal warehouse on the Sound. Has PNA decals on it. That's on, uh, state route 525, south of Paine Air Force Base. You might have them assemble at the base."

"That would work fine," the official replied. "How do you use this thing?"

Bolan showed him how, then he showed the battle cruiser her heading and began making tracks northward.

It was time once again for her to earn her keep.

This time, with her claws.

17: TACTICS

Sure—corner the money market and rape the world. The guys had been looking for a handle for years, and maybe now they'd found it. *The Thing of all the Things*—the big hit—the clout to end all clouts—*financial domination of the entire civilized world!*

It could be done. Bolan knew it could. He didn't know *how*, but he knew that it *could*. In this country alone it required an entire department of government just to keep the *legitimate* giants from taking over and gobbling all the little people, destroying competition, rigging markets, gouging the consumer for all he could stand.

Take that same type of superbusinessmen and give them the Mafia mentality, spread them across the globe in a multinational network of financial manipulations that could reach into every monetary system, every national and international market—give them the absolute, raw power that comes from the control of economic life or death for entire industries and whole nations—and what do you have?—sure, you have *Cosa di tutti Cosi*.

They'd been dreaming of it ever since Capone—nibbling at it with guys like Cohen and Lansky—now, somehow, by some handle, by some freakish turn of world circumstances, they'd managed to

147

actually start putting it together. Apparently they had the kicker. But what was it? The worldwide energy crisis? The international crunch in virtually every critical commodity? The paralysis of international inflation? The contagion of political crises in just about every nation of the world?

Was that combination of circumstances the kicker? —or was it, conversely, an *immediately visible effect* of a take-over *already in progress?*

Was the creation of a secret super world bank the next logical step in the pattern?—or was it simply another kicker?

The cross-town conversation in Bolan's war machine was concerned with those considerations, and more.

Brognola told the others, "It hurts my brain, I don't want to think about it any more right now."

To which Leo Turrin retorted, "You've just got battle fatigue from round one, in Washington. It won't help to close your eyes and retire to a neutral corner. The mob boys love that—they'll just swagger over and keep on kicking the shit out of you."

Tiredly, Brognola admitted, "Okay, so I'm getting neurotic. Haven't had a decent night's sleep in months. Striker—what are *you* thinking? How far has the thing gone? How much time is left?"

"I have the easy part," Bolan muttered.

"How's that?"

"I don't have to think about it. You call me Striker. Right? You don't call me Thinker."

"That simple, eh?"

"For me, yeah. There's inductive and deductive logic—right? One form generalizes from particulars. The other particularizes from generalities. In my language, that's simply the difference between strategy and tactics. You guys handle the strategies. Right now I'm busy as hell with tactics."

Brognola and Turrin exchanged glances.

Turrin grinned.

Brognola said, as though Bolan were not present, "Sometimes I dislike that son of a bitch."

"You envy him," Turrin argued.

"Same difference," Brognola replied, sighing. "I'd just like to go kick the shit out of somebody, myself."

Turrin said, "He's right, you know. We're sitting here trying to solve the problems of the world. But the only problem we can touch is right here. Right, Sarge?"

Bolan commented, "Even right here, all we can do is try."

Brognola asked him, "What do you expect to find in that warehouse, Tactician? Not gold or silver, surely."

Bolan smiled thinly. "No. But maybe the logistics for it."

"Oh hell, now he's a logistician," Brognola growled.

Bolan chuckled. "I've been holding out on you guys. I do have some rather heady stuff to tell you. But first I want a look inside that warehouse."

Turrin said, "This is where the contraband has been going. Right?"

Bolan nodded. "Martialing area, anyway, I think. It has been moving on, I'd say quite steadily. But I want a look-see. I believe those shipping manifests were generally correct. I think it's been mostly machinery. The *kind* of machinery nobody wants traced to its ultimate use. Most of that stuff I'd think they could have picked up here in this country—maybe even locally. Take those weapons, now. It's a special case, sure, but the same logic applies. Hell, they were *made* in this country. But look at the route they took

149

to Puget Sound. Legally exported to Europe. Exchanged through three different legitimate brokers before finally disappearing from view. Then they pop up here, in a marine crate marked for Expo '74."

"For most stuff," Turrin said, "there'd be no tracks, no tracks at all."

"Yeah. Super secret. These guys are sparing no effort, in that sense. You'll see why, if I can tie it all together."

"But don't call him *Thinker*," Brognola said, smiling.

"What's the big mystery, Sarge?" asked Turrin. "A new gold mine in Alaska?"

Bolan chuckled and said, "That may not be far wrong, either. If our people ever start hauling that oil from the new fields up there, anyone sitting here on Puget Sound is going to be in a hell of a good position to cash in on all sorts of trade. That's what built Seattle in the first place."

"Commerce, huh?" Brognola said.

"Yeah, sure," said Turrin. "Or harassment."

"Why would anybody want to harass that?" Brognola asked disgustedly.

"Are you crazy?" Turrin shot back. "That's the favorite occupation of the nickel and dime boys."

"We're not talking about nickels and dimes."

"How do you think they got to the *Cosa?*" Turrin argued. "Numbers, bimboes, protection, smack, alcohol, vending machines, pinballs, jukes, bandits—you name a nickel or a dime, I'll give you the name of the guy that rolled it into a million dollar territory."

"Sure, sure—but I'm saying that none of that anywhere approaches the magnitude of potential commerce from millions of barrels of crude a day."

It was a pointless argument, and both seemed to realize it—but on it went.

"Ah hell, they play both sides of the street, Hal—you know that. One guy's territory is commerce, the other guy's is knockdowns. As an example, look what Luciano did with the—"

"Hell, forget Luciano. That's old history. It's the *now* that counts."

"It's the now I'm talking about. Luciano's empire didn't die with the man. Just look at . . ."

Bolan turned off the banter from the friendly antagonists, recognizing it as sheer nervous release.

Both these men spent their lives balanced precariously on the edge of a knifeblade. This was probably the first chance in months for either to let the hair down a bit, to unwind just a turn.

Bolan ordinarily translated his own tensions into action.

These guys had to sit and fester with it.

Which was another reason why Bolan would accept no concept of "secret portfolio"—undercover sanction and amnesty for past "crimes." He'd play his game his way, thanks, for as long as the game could last. And he would die the way he'd lived—with blood on his hands and unpardoned scars on the soul.

The American writer Elbert Hubbard had once observed: "God will not look you over for medals, degrees or diplomas, but for scars."

Bolan would carry his own scars to his own judgment.

Right now he was simply trying to carry them to the next zone of combat. And the going was getting rough, with the interstate route now behind him and the atmosphere out there getting thicker with every turn of the wheels.

Brognola and Turrin suddenly became aware of Bolan's intense concentration into the problems of navigation. They fell silent; Turrin chewing on his cigar, the man from "paradise" bent forward and massaging his knuckles as he peered into the misty shrouds of that night in "that other" Washington.

It was to be one which none of them would ever forget.

18: FIRETRACK

The impressive vehicle was totally darkened, engine idling quietly, sitting just in off the road at about dead center, maybe fifty yards from the building.

As warehouses go, it seemed small. Floodlights marked the corners at roof level but were barely visible in the choking mists.

"I can't see a damned thing," Leo Turrin complained.

"Relax," Brognola suggested.

"It's two thirty. He's been out there about ten minutes."

"He knows what he's doing."

"Sure."

Both men were peering tensely through the wet windshield. Brognola's .38 lay on the seat beside him. Turrin was not armed. He said, "He's right, you know. This *is* his element. Me, I have two left feet. And I even get dizzy in my own bedroom if all the lights are out."

"Relax, Leo. That's a hell of a man out there. He knows what he's doing."

"Hell, I know that. I just wish *I* knew what he's doing."

"I'd settle for knowing *why*," Brognola said. "What d'you suppose he's really stumbled onto, Leo?"

"It could be anything. The guy has an uncanny sense of things. All he needs to get started is a smell."

"I'm just afraid he got quite a nose full, this time."

"Looks that way, doesn't it. Do you really think . . . ?"

Brognola sighed heavily and turned away from the glass. "Hell, I don't know, Leo. I'm getting so I don't trust my own guts anymore. They're tied up so often, over so much—sometimes I wonder if I've just gone full paranoid and the rest of the world is really sane and beautiful."

"Well, sure, a guy gets to that. But I don't think you're paranoid, Hal."

"From one suspect to another, eh? Thanks for nothing."

Turrin chuckled.

A misty draft swirled into the vehicle. Brognola scooped up the .38 and whirled smoothly toward the midsection then relaxed with a relieved sigh as a black-clad figure materialized there and the door slid shut.

"Home is the scout," Turrin greeted him. "What's the lie out there?"

The federal official holstered his pistol and stepped back to make room for Bolan's entry into the cockpit.

The "scout" dropped into the command chair and immediately began doing things at the mini-console. "Very close out there," he reported. "Visibility's about five feet, and I'm giving that the benefit of some doubt. Here's the setup. It's a hard house. No windows. No personnel doors. Just a big cargo door at the center, roll type, big enough to admit a semi-trailer. Similar door on the water side. Short pier over there for smallcraft. Very quiet, all around."

Brognola asked, "Did you get inside?"

"Not yet." Bolan was flipping switches, operating levers. A viewplate about the size of a small portable television screen swung into position, glowing reddishly. "Guard shack just outside the rolldoor," he continued. "There was a sentry in there, a Franciscus type."

"Was?" Turrin asked absently, gazing with interest at the glowing screen.

"Yeah, was. And there's still a vehicle at the end of the building, north side. People inside but I didn't try for a headcount. It's a crew, though."

Brognola tapped the viewplate and asked, "What's this thing?"

"Monitor for the optics capability," Bolan explained. "Watch, now, and I'll give you a look at that guardshack."

He punched a button and made a lever adjustment. A resolution of focus resulted, then a small reddish beam appeared at center screen. After another minor adjustment, the front wall of the warehouse appeared in a weirdly red-tinged circle, then the guardhouse leapt into resolution.

"Be damned," Turrin muttered. "Infra-red."

"Laser-supplemented," Bolan said.

"How far can you see with that thing?" Brognola wondered.

"In this atmosphere, that's about maximum range. I can get a mile in reasonably dry air."

"I've heard of these," the official said. "Some police agencies are getting into it. On a smaller scale, I would imagine—nothing this elaborate."

Turrin said, "People out there don't even know you're spotlighting them."

"Not unless they have receptors," Bolan said. He was busy at another set of controls. "Seeing's nice, but it's not always enough. I'm going to—Hal, you

155

may not want to be around while this is happening. Step into the toilet if you'd rather not."

"To hell with that," Brognola growled. "I'm staying."

The JD official was "staying" for a rather mind-boggling demonstration of the warwagon's combat capabilities.

A rocket launcher was built into the roof of the vehicle—normally retracted and concealed from view beneath flush-fit panels. Upon command from below, the motorized swivel-platform raised and locked into position for firing.

Targeting was entirely controlled from the command position below, operating through electronic circuitry tied into the regular optics system. A floor-mounted, foot-controlled device which Bolan labeled "a rock-and-press trackfire" provided control of both targeting and firing without using the hands.

Reloading, Bolan explained, was not practicable during the heat of combat, though. It was a "four-shot system." Within that limitation, however, a guy with a supple ankle and a steady foot could unleash considerable destruction.

Bolan brought the system on line by depressing the "Fire Enable" button on his miniconsole. A small amber light began flashing, in an indication that the launch platform was being raised. As it locked into place, a green light signalled that event and immediately the optics were taken over by the Fire Control System. Rangemarks then became superimposed on the viewscreen, and the system was "Go."

Explaining the operations in terse reportage to his companions as he went through the steps, Bolan rocked the floor control into azimuth and range corrections, centering the rangemarks on the warehouse door.

"Last chance to tell it goodbye," he said quietly.

Turrin muttered. "I will be damned. How do you fire it?"

"Like this," Bolan replied. He banged his knee with a fist. A "whoosh" and momentary brightness signalled the departure of the "hot bird." It flashed into the foreground of the viewscreen and whizzed straight along the horizontal beam on a tail of flame to impact almost immediately on target with thunder and considerable lightning. That heavy atmosphere out there was momentarily torn by a flash that briefly illuminated the mists with white-hot incandescence and set the night trembling into retreat.

Brognola growled, "I'm impressed." It was an understatement. He could not look away. As viewed through the optics, great puffing flame-lined clouds had replaced the warehouse door as well as substantial adjacent areas.

And the "picture" was changing rapidly now as Bolan realigned targeting on a starboard scan—halting suddenly, correcting and centering on the nose of a vehicle just then emerging at high speed around the corner of the building.

Bolan thumped his knee again to depress the foot-control, and another whizzer streaked along that tunnel of red light. With the resultant flash in the target zone, electrified faces flared into high resolution for perhaps one flashing impulse of electronic vision before disappearing into eternity behind another firecloud.

Leo Turrin wheeled away from that with a queasy, "My God!"

"*Their* God," Bolan growled fiercely. "Let it eat them."

A martialing area, sure. Also, if the evidence could be correctly read, some sort of an assembly plant.

Empty crates and cartons were stacked almost to the ceiling at one end of the building. At the other end were greasy work benches, heavy tools scattered about, chain lifts, equipment dollies. Elsewhere scattered throughout the building were unopened crates of various sizes, all stacked in neat rows, each of which were identified by crude, hand-lettered signs attached to the end cases.

Brognola was poking about the "unopened" area, taking notes.

Turrin had gone with Bolan to the "trash area" for an assessment of the empties.

Bolan remarked, "I'm more interested in what has already moved through here."

Turrin agreed with that and pointed to a heavy crate near the bottom of the pile. "Air compressor," he noted. "What the hell would they want with a compressor that big?"

Bolan shrugged and said, "Maybe they're planning some underwater work," and continued on with a systematic visual scan of the evidence. Not all the boxes were marked, but enough were that a pattern began very quickly to emerge. He took Turrin by the arm and growled, "That's enough for me. Let's go."

As they rejoined, Brognola kicked a large, flat crate on the floor beside him and remarked, "Here's our bank. Or part of it. That one box must weigh a ton or more. Know what it is? Door for a vault."

"Bingo," Turrin said solemnly.

All three men seemed a bit awed by their discoveries. They were standing beside a handmade placard which had been thumbtacked to a shipping skid, identifying "Security Components."

158

Brognola said, "Looks like you're batting a thousand, Striker. They're building something, somewhere, that's for sure."

Bolan replied, "They're building Langley Island."

"Where is that?"

"Within a rifle shot of here," Bolan said. "Let's go back into the wagon. Want to show you something."

He took the men to his plot table and first showed them the chart of Puget Sound, relating the island to the overall area—quite insignificant, really. Then he showed aerial photos taken from Grimaldi's first overflight and, finally, the sketches he'd made during the soft penetration.

Bolan did not ordinarily work this way—in cahoots with the law. He'd made occasional exceptions to that rule, of course, and this time was a very important exception. Too much was at stake here to stand on personal game rules.

"They're still excavating over there," he pointed out. "The room I was in is obviously a command bunker of some type. I should have looked further while I was there. There could be a dozen rooms completed and ready for use. These tunnels go off from there like the spokes of a wheel. If you'll note some of the angles they make, it would certainly suggest more vaults either completed or planned. They've moved a lot of watertight stuff, air compressors and the like that could even suggest airlocks for tunnels out into the Sound!"

"I wonder . . . I just wonder," Brognola mused. "Could they use subs to make underwater transfers?"

Bolan shrugged. "Why not? It sounds wild, I know —but the whole damn idea is wild, so why pose limits?"

Turrin said, "Right. For that matter, they could be putting vaults right out there under the water.

159

Why not, eh? What could be better than a secret bank beneath the waters of Puget Sound?"

Brognola muttered, "How much of a work force do they have out there?"

Bolan shook his head. "I don't know, Hal. The only people actually staying on the island are the hard force. I did get a bit of intel that leads me to believe that they've even brought their workers in from somewhere outside the country."

"Sandhogs," Turrin said. "It would take pro's for this."

"Must have some good powder men, too," Brognola observed. "There's plenty of the stuff stored here."

"Good thing it wasn't stored by the door," Turrin said with a chuckle.

Bolan cocked an eyebrow and asked, "How much powder?"

"Oh hell, I'd say . . . tons, maybe. How much is in a keg?"

Bolan shrugged. "I've never used it in that form."

"Well there's twenty kegs to those crates." Brognola glanced at his notebook. "I just made a rough estimate on the number of crates. I guessed forty."

Bolan said, "That's interesting."

"How interesting?" Brognola asked.

"There must be a good supply on the island, too."

"Are you thinking what I think you're thinking?"

Bolan smiled. "There has to be a solution, Hal."

"I guess I better call my marshals in," Brognola decided. "I don't know about you two, but I've had enough of this place."

Bolan said, "We still have a lot to discuss, Hal. But you may as well get the guys started. In this weather, it will take them a while to get here."

Brognola nodded and moved forward to the mobile phone. Turrin called after him, "Have 'em bring a meat wagon, too. I counted four bodies out there, in bits and pieces." He turned to Bolan with a sigh. "Hal's pretty well shaken by all this. I guess you've noticed that, too. Theories are one thing. Seeing is something else. How do you really read this, Mack?"

"It's the Thing, all right," Bolan quietly replied.

"I'm sure it is, yeah. I didn't mean that. I mean, what the hell do you *do* about it? It's already beyond Hal. He knows it, and that's what has hold of his guts. He needs a naval task force, not a platoon of marshals."

"Hal stays clear until I'm done," Bolan said frostily. "That understanding is implicit any time we come together. You know that."

"Sure. You do have a plan, then."

"Yeah."

"Mind if I ask . . . ?"

"If I get lucky," Bolan told him, "I'll blow the whole works out of the water. That won't turn the world around, exactly, but at least it'll confuse the hell out of things for a while. In the meantime, maybe Hal and his people can get something going."

Leo Turrin was not convinced. "Hey, you know, we're all in this. I mean, it's my world, too. I got a wife and kids, right? And this thing is just too big. Too big, Mack. I think you should let Hal skull it through from here."

Bolan stubbornly shook his head. "I don't know whose world it is, Leo, but it's *my* game. Hal will get completely bogged down with the legalities of the thing. Meanwhile the enemy dances lightly away and pops up again another day to try again. No. I've got to show them the cost, Leo. And it has to be heavy."

"Yeah," Turrin said, grudgingly agreeing.

161

"How about those two hundred hardmen? Where are they?"

"Stashed around town somewhere. We've got a meet for eight o'clock this morning. Not the Indians, just the chiefs. But they were all checked in before midnight."

"Do you know any of those troops, Leo? I mean, *know*."

Turrin shook his head in a slow negative. "Not even the chiefs. I gather they were all recruited directly by Franciscus. He has the Seattle contract for your head, by the way. Combat guy. I guess he's dangerous. The old men love him."

"Get those guys on the island for me, Leo. Get them there before dawn. *All* of them."

"What? You crazy? If you're—oh! I get. Clean sweep, eh?"

"That's the general idea. So far I'm not sure how. But can you *get* them there?"

"Oh, well . . . that's *my* element, Tactician." Turrin grinned sourly. "I'll get them there. All I have to do is tell the truth, or shades of it."

"Here's a kicker for you. You can show Franciscus the minipak I implanted on the roof. Parapet, outside railing, south wall. Also the whole joint is strung with micropickups. But dammit, Leo—don't go on too strong. This guy is pretty sharp."

"Yeah, well, let me worry about the hard things. You take care of the easy ones. Go blow up the damn island, will you?"

"She blows at dawn," Bolan promised.

19: DOMINO SET

Leo Turrin bit down savagely on his cigar and spoke around it via the side of his mouth to snarl, "What the hell is this, guy? Don't tell me you're laying around here on your dead ass in fancy pajamas while this Bolan is romping all over your town!"

The Captain could not believe his ears. He shook a sleep-fogged head, zeroing attention onto his executive officer, Harve Mathews. "What is this, Harve? Who is this guy? Get him out of here!"

"This is Mr. Turrin, Captain—our liaison. He insisted—I didn't know—he says it's urgent. Just busted right in."

"I'm gonna bust some asses, too," Turrin raged on. "I never saw such a disgraceful—what kind of a junior commando outfit is this, anyway? Get outta that fuckin' bed, you looneytune! The fuckin' guy is taking your whole thing apart for you!"

Franciscus threw back the covers and leapt to his feet. "What?" he howled.

"You don't lay on your ass while this guy's in town! He'll jerk it right out from under you while you're liftin' your leg to pee! While you lay here sleeping in fancy pajamas, he's got the whole damned joint wired for sound! Don't you ever shake it down? Don't you have any goddam electronic security, for crissakes!"

163

Franciscus was stunned, dazed by the verbal attack. He directed a wavery gaze toward Mathews and commanded, "Coffee, Harve. Lace it good. Give some to the mouth here, too. Then sound reveille. Roll everybody out."

"Mr. Turrin has people running all over the penthouse," the exec reported as he moved toward a bar in the corner of the bedroom.

"He has what?"

"Damn right!" the liaison shouted. "We're shaking you down, jake! I was told that you limberdicks out here knew what you were doing! Listen, boy scouts in my town know better." He tossed a small, plasticized sphere, roughly the size of a quarter, onto the bed. "I walked right in outta the cold and picked that off one of your chandeliers! You know what that is, dammit? Do you know?"

"Bugged!" the Captain said in a hollow voice.

Turrin cried, "Ahhh shit!" and swaggered to the window, stuck both hands in his pockets, and turned his back to it all.

He had the guy shook, yeah. It could be an unnerving experience, awakening to something like that. It'd happened to Leo Turrin a time or two; he knew.

He lit his cigar and gazed into the night for a while, giving the "elite" time to compose themselves. When he turned back to them, Franciscus was dressed in pants and shirt, had a cigarette going, held a coffee cup in one hand and Bolan's bug in the other. Mathews stood stiffly to the side, eyes on the floor.

In a much milder tone, Turrin called over, "Ay. I'm sorry, eh. I shouldn't come in like that. I get too excited. Sorry if I fucked up the protocol or what

164

d'you call it. But hey, I've had my boys out for hours, running this thing down."

"What do you mean?" Franciscus asked, the voice crisp, now—but not unfriendly.

Turrin waved the cigar in a circle and moved slowly back to the center of the room. "I can't expect a guy with your—I mean, you know, my boys knew all that crap before they got ten years old. Otherwise they'd never reached ten years old. Know what I mean? Street ways. You should get your boys to shaking this joint. Check the window ledges, inside and out. Even the walls outside. This's a top floor— right? Better check the roof. There's a relay rig somewhere around here."

"How do you know that for sure?" Franciscus barked.

"Common sense would be enough," Turrin replied loftily. "But I got more than that to go on. It's all over the damn streets."

"*What* is?"

Turrin's tagman poked head and shoulders through the doorway and called in, "Hey boss."

"Come on in, Jocko."

The little guy had his hands cupped together, bearing a near overflow of quarter-size gadgets. He stepped up and deposited them on the bed, then went to stand behind his boss before reporting, "Chick sends it. He says he thinks it's clean now."

The Franciscus gaze jerked away from the embarrassing evidence. "*What* is all over the streets?" he asked, the voice dimming again.

"You have a guy named Helmann up here last night?"

A sick look briefly transited that military countenance.

Mathews jerked noticeably.

Turrin said, "Sure you did. The local cops know it. The feds know it. The whole damn town by now knows it. Bolan blitzed in here sometime last night and wired you. He recorded you and the Helmann guy in dark conference. The feds have that conversation, Johnny."

"Find that transmitter, Harve," the Captain quietly commanded.

Mathews moved quickly out of the room.

Franciscus showed his visitor a strained smile and said, "Well. I've heard of you, Leo. Mostly good. I'm very impressed. Just sorry to meet you for the first time with egg all over my face."

"It beats shit," Turrin replied, smiling sourly. "After a brush with this guy Bolan, most boys come off looking more that way—shitfaced, I mean. Look, it's your show. The men told me to stand by and assist. But you better do something quick. What's this I'm hearing about an island?"

The military gaze retracted then lashed across that room and seized Leo Turrin's lips. "What did you say?"

"God, you have a hearin' problem? You know what I said, dammit. My sources say that Bolan knows. He *knows,* guy. Have you studied this boy?"

"Not in depth, no. Nobody expected him to pop up here so soon. I'm getting a profile run on—"

"You better forget the damn profiles and concentrate on the *guy.* He *has* popped, see. And you better start scrambling. You better grab your balls. Translation: take care of the things you prize the most. The guy will be laying all over you before daylight. Take it from one who's been laid enough already to know."

Franciscus snapped an anguished gaze to his wristwatch. He whirled and went to the window. "He couldn't know," he muttered. "Nobody knows."

"The *street* knows, Johnny."

"Did the old men tell you about the island?"

"I never heard of it until an hour ago."

"What did you hear?"

"Just that. An island somewhere. Bolan hiring himself a fast boat. He's prepping an assault of some kind. Buying weapons. Big ones. You better get set, bub. Or else tell me and let me. The men sent me out here for one damn reason. Protect the investment. We know what this boy can do. They sent me because I know how. Now I can't go back there and tell them I stood here and watched you piss it all away."

"You'll tell them *nothing!*" Franciscus snarled.

Turrin rocked on the balls of his feet and turned a deliberate gaze onto his tagman. "Tell the boys we go," he ordered.

The little guy nodded uncertainly and hurried out.

Turrin told the quivering Captain, "I don't work for you, bub. It's the other way around. You keep your ass in your hand and remember who pays your goddam bills. Either you got a firm grip or you ain't. If you have, then you guide that ass out of here and you by Jesus get something to moving. I mean *now!*"

It was obvious that Captain Franciscus was not accustomed to this kind of talking-to.

The muscles of his jaw were twitching and the eyes were blazing mad.

Harve Mathews loped into the room, defusing that confrontation with a breathless report.

"Got it! Had a hunch, Cap—that helicopter. Found it right there!" He was holding out a small box that could have been a cigarette case with a tiny antenna projecting from the top.

Either it was the final straw, or it served as an excellent face-saver for the Captain.

"Sound the alert, condition red!" he snapped. "Call the bosun, get the boats fired up! Reveille those new men, send some cars! I want a full formation at the pier within thirty minutes! Alert the armorer, get a truck to the pier, full combat weapons and rounds for two hundred men! Call the island! Talk to Presley personally. Tell him to double the patrols on the beaches! Get a weather report! Okay, move it!"

"That sounds more like it," Turrin said, sighing, as the executive officer double-timed it out of there.

"We know how to handle a situation," the Captain sneered. "Tell *that* to your old men."

Turrin swept out of the penthouse with his crew in tow, entirely pleased with himself. He would, of course, tell the old men nothing. The "hard work" was over. The rest would be up to Bolan . . . and his direct solution to a very complex problem.

At that very moment, Harold Brognola was working a complex problem of his own, in the duty officer's office at the Bremerton Naval Barracks.

"You tell your C.O. that I'll have complete verification via the Pentagon—or the Joint Chiefs, if that's what he wants—before a single boat moves. Meanwhile, though, I want the cogs turning. If I don't have at least ten amphibians on the line and ready to roar in thirty minutes, somebody's tit will end up in a very tight ringer. You tell him that."

"Yes sir. The C.O. understands the urgency, sir. He'll be here personally in ten minutes, sir."

Brognola glowered at the young ensign for a moment, then clasped his hands together and moved away from there.

The weather was beginning to break. Forecast

168

calling for an early general lifting, entire coastal regions.

Some break!

Tit in the ringer? It would be cock n' balls n' all, Brognola's—not somebody's—if Bolan didn't pull the thing just right.

God! Tactician, hell! The guy was carrying the whole burden, all of it. And all the nation's third cop could do was pace and sweat.

20: HARD TOUCH

"Wish I could talk you out of this," Grimaldi groused. "You're even losing your weather cover. Ceiling's up to about a hundred feet now, in spots. NAS says rapid clearing."

"Worry about getting yourself in and out, Jack. If you think you can't, say so. We'll consider an alternative. But I am getting in there."

"Hell I can get in and out. I've taken these babes down in the middle of enemy encirclements many times. That's not the point. The point is—"

"I have to get in, Jack. That's the point."

"Okay, okay."

The little chopper was specially prepped for the mission. The personnel door on Bolan's side had been removed and left behind. His seat was gone, as well as a section of floor and outer skin beneath his feet.

Bolan was now crouched at the edge of the hole, gazing down through the skids at the choppy waters of Puget Sound. He was rigged for heavy combat, armed to the teeth, burdened with a load nearly equal to his own weight.

A backpack alone hauled fifty pounds of "goop"— plastic explosives. Double utility belts crossed the chest, supporting dangling grenades and other munitions of blazing warfare.

The .44 AutoMag rode position of honor at his

right hip. Numerous reload clips for the weapon were grouped to either side of the holster within easy reach.

Head weapon for the mission was Bolan's favorite heavy piece—the M-16/M-79 over n' under combo. The '16 spat a hot trail of 5.56 mm tumblers in auto or could be fired as a semiauto. The '79 was a hard-punch piece, breechloaded and versatile, handling rounds of high explosive, fragmentation, smoke, gas, flare, or double-aught buck. With any load, she was hell in hand. For the moment, the double weapon was strapped across the back of his shoulders, secured.

Grimaldi fiddled with his headset and announced, "Ceiling now is one fifty and sloping high. We'll have to drop through at least two hundred feet of clear to set you down. It's going to be tense."

Bolan replied, "I leave it to you, Jack. Scrub it if you must."

"No, hell no. I'll get you in. Rather do it this way than drop you from four thousand feet." He chuckled nervously. "I was always a sucker for grunts, especially you teeth-baring gung-ho types. I'm climbing up top, now. We're getting close."

Bolan smiled at the guy in complete understanding, then began mentally reorienting himself to the lie down there.

A moment later the phones crackled with a report on the air/ground channel. "Low Boy to High Boy. Anybody there?"

It was Leo Turrin, in the warwagon.

Grimaldi punched the channel selector and gave Bolan a visual go-ahead.

"Go ahead, Low Boy," Bolan replied.

"Okay, they're sprung and scrambling. Give it about one hour from this moment for them to organize and get there."

Bolan punched the mark on his wrist chronometer. "Roger, understand one hour from now. Thanks, Low Boy. We're going."

"That's good. I'm about went. Now moving the vehicle to backdrop position."

"Roger."

"Tally ho, man."

"Thanks, stay hard."

Grimaldi returned the setup to intercom and asked, "Who's our friend?"

"Best left nameless, Jack," Bolan replied.

"Gotcha. Okay, get set. We should be about a thousand yards uprange. 'Bout time to hit that flare. Your wind is . . . yeah, okay, right on our tail. Let it go at my mark."

Bolan extended a flarepistol through the open doorway.

"Mark!"

The pyrotechnic whizzed off in a straight-horizontal trajectory, headed upwind. It had a long fuse. In a moment, the parachute would open and the flare would descend far to their rear, breaking the cloud cover over water and coming down on the forward shore. Hopefully. It was purely a diversionary move. Bolan intended to set down in the quiet area to the rear. He simply wanted a brief moment with most eyes on that island directed the other way.

Grimaldi was now executing a wide circle and losing altitude rapidly.

Bolan poised himself at the opening in the floor and reported, "Headset coming off, Jack. I'll be on visual."

"Right. Watch yourself. I'll give you all the running room I can. But drop at your own discretion. Your view will probably be better than mine. Good luck, man. Like the guy said, tally-ho."

Bolan snatched off the headset and raised a fist to his flying friend. Then he bent headfirst through the floor opening, steadying himself outside by a skid strut.

The mists dissolved in a flash. Land appeared, darkly. Buildings rose up in fuzzy outline.

Far ahead, brilliance was breaking the cloud cover and descending in a gentle float through open skies.

The little craft lurched, rose slightly, dropped greatly, lurched again—then spinning and side-slipping in a steady drop. Earth was whizzing by. Fencing flashed past, barely off the skids. Bolan launched himself, seizing the skid in both hands as though it were a parallel bar at the neighborhood gym, swinging, now hanging vertically. Toes dragged slightly—legs pistoned up with knees bent, and he let go.

He hit the earth running, then stumbled under the momentum with too much weight—fell—slid to rest.

Already the chopper was out of sight, its sounds a distant thumping upon the night.

Bolan pulled himself to a crouch and tested his working parts.

All systems were go. No hurt more serious than a skinned knee. All weaponry intact. Those plastics, thank the fates, still inert.

Things were happening up front, though. People in fast movement, shouts, the coughing of an outboard motor. The diversion was working.

He jogged toward the sounds, thudding at every step with the extra weight, then broke toward the cover of the buildings.

Other feet thudded ahead. Bolan stepped into the lee of the building and froze.

A voice, pretty close, called out, "Okay, but I swear I heard a chopper!"

Said another, obviously a leader with rank, "You'll be hearing a bullet in the belly if you don't follow orders! Get out there and back up those beach defenses!"

The feet thudded away.

A radio, directly ahead, squawked briefly with some unintelligible message.

That leadership voice responded. "Wilco, I already did. Compound's about stripped clean though, Jerry. I'd hate to have to handle any serious threat in here."

Another squawk, then the reply: "Roger. Be glad when they get here."

So would Bolan. The mighty 200. Not, however, until he had properly prepared their reception.

He'd be preparing nothing whatever if he remained pinned here. He moved on. That guy up there was no more than an indistinct shadow in a deeper shadow when he suddenly stiffened and turned in half-visible profile, with Bolan still several paces back.

"Got a light?" Bolan asked casually.

"Who the hell is that?" the guy demanded, irritably startled.

Bolan hit him from two paces out with a judo kick to the groin and a simultaneous straight arm to the throat. The soldier went down with a faint squawk as the only sound. Bolan finished the silent job with a nylon garrote, pinning the victim with his knees as he took key ring and radio then moved quickly on.

No—there would be no soft touches on this visit. This one was for keeps.

Another lone human barrier stood quietly at the front of the center building, head cocked slightly to one side as though listening intently to distant sounds, his back to Bolan.

175

The Executioner called over, "Hey!" and the guy spun around just in time to catch the stiletto in his throat. He dropped his auto and stood there bug-eyed, hands to his throat, then toppled over.

Bolan stepped over to the door, found the proper key, and pushed inside. A battery lantern at the head of the stairs was throwing a soft light. He moved the two dead soldiers in there and left them in a dark corner, then took the lantern and descended toward the mission goal.

Ten minutes later, Bolan was completely satisfied that he knew all the secrets of the installation—all that were readable, at any rate. The work was no-where near half-completed. Three large chambers had been hollowed out, one beneath each building. Only the central chamber was at any degree of fin-ished work. Tunnels ran off at a dozen angles from the central core but led nowhere—perhaps one day they would have.

He found a supply shaft above the room that lay beneath the east building—and up there, in that building, he located the main powder storage.

And yeah, Hal old worry wart, there was a bundle on hand.

Then began the arduous and time-consuming task of moving the TNT into position for the big event.

At forty minutes past touch down he was shaping plastic detonators and implanting time fuses. He ran out of numbers during this period, knew it, but kept on until the task was complete.

It would be daylight up there now, or at least the early stages of the transition from night to day.

If the weather-guessers were right this time, there would be no more heavy atmosphere except for a thin layer relatively high.

Grimmest of all—the Terrible 200 should now be

on board. And there sat Bolan in an underground vault, with many tons of TNT for company, set to go in a matter of minutes.

He regrouped himself in the central control room, chose his weapons with care, balancing delicately the trade-off of weight versus effect, and made himself ready.

At precisely sixty-five minutes into the mission, he erupted onto the grounds of that joint with the bellowing '79 poised and ready.

If the Fates watched over angels and fools, Bolan did not have to wonder about his particular category of care.

Striding across those grounds not 20 yards up-range, coming down between the bungalows, was Captain Johnny himself and retinue—five of them in close military stride and clipping it off smartly.

They spotted Bolan at about the same moment that his trigger-finger reacted to the situation.

Quick reactors they were, but not quick enough—startled surprise blending smoothly into evasive choreography with bodies flinging in every direction as the big piece boomed and heaved 40 millimeters of hellfire into the midst of them, adding a new dimension to the dance and a new movement to the overture.

He caught a glimpse of Franciscus through the firecloud, rolling and flopping to rest against a bungalow—but then another party came pounding around the corner of the big house.

He swung into that one with the '16 ablaze and hurtling lightning, scattering people in another crazed dance for survival.

Then, suddenly, soldiers were pouring in from everywhere—through the back door of the house, from bungalows, and from every perimeter.

177

Right—the numbers were off and the 200 were on —and Bolan the Bold had bought himself a belly buster this time.

He hit them with gas, and smoke, and HE, and tumblers—he hit them with snorting .44s and grenades—and he gave them all the war he'd been able to bring with him, laying down finally a billowing curtain of chemical smoke behind which a tactically retreating soldier boy may sprint like hell.

And he was doing so—lungs turning to solid blood and legs going to lead when the heartening *whomp* of rotary blades overhead reassured him that Jack the Birdman had come through again.

The swooping eagle came in across his quarter in a calculated intercept, moving a bit faster than Bolan would have desired—but then so were those others to the rear.

He caught the skid on his chest with the last leap left in him. It jerked into the armpits with wrenching pain as unequal momentums came into balance— then he was swinging clear—man and machine becoming united in common flight as they lifted up, up, and away.

The whole thing must have been as mind-blowing to those left behind as to the man dangling from the eagle's talons—or else it was all just too demoralizing to encourage further effort from the ground; not another round came after him—and with the way Grimaldi was balling it, there wasn't much time for the ground crews to get it back together in time, anyway.

They were a mile downrange before Bolan got himself together and got it aboard—then it finally took a helping hand from the man at the stick for that last pull onto solid support.

Bolan lay there panting for a moment, then he

178

drew himself clear of the hole in the floor and sat there watching his hands quiver until Grimaldi tossed him a headset. He donned it, and the damn guy was saying. "Where the hell you been goofing off the past ten minutes, dammit? I came in at count sixty and I came back at count sixty-five. Then I got curious about all the smoke at count seventy and figured I'd give 'er one last swoop. We can go back and try it again, though, if you demand perfection."

"Get screwed, you beautiful bastard," Bolan panted.

The fantastic flyboy laughed for outrageous joy and sent the hot little bird circling back the way they'd come.

"How much fuse time is left?" he asked.

Bolan tired to hold his trembling hand still long enough to read the time, then couldn't focus his eyes, finally giving it up to reply, "Couldn't be long now."

"I hope not," the pilot said, still chuckling. "Look below."

Bolan really did not wish to. He was quite content to be where he was, but he leaned forward to peer through the hole and immediately said "Brognola's navy."

A solid wave of a dozen or more U.S. Navy landing craft was cutting wide wakes toward Langley Island.

Grimaldi laughed and said, "I'm going to miss you, guy, if you ever retire. This is my second eagle's cyc view of a big boom with you."

The guy was talking about the energy storm over Texas.

Bolan sighed and asked, "How's the visibility?"

"Come up and see."

He tried his legs and found them operable, com-

179

ing up into a crouch at the instrument panel. The bird was hovering. Langley Island was dead ahead about two thousand yards and maybe a thousand feet below. Bolan's vision cleared and his other physical systems went into second-go. He glanced at the watch. "Countdown," he announced to the pilot. "Thirty seconds to boom."

Grimaldi lit a cigarette and handed it to the hellfire guy.

Bolan accepted it and took a careful drag, favoring the raw lungs, watching intently a countdown to the destruction of some men's dream, some men's nightmare.

It was a weird blow. Things moved down there, as in an earthquake and by no other means—no fire, no smoke, just movement. Three buildings collapsed and disappeared momentarily, then spewed forth upon trumpeting streamers of fire and smoke—the sound wave arrived along with that and rocked the whirlybird—a long series of rumbling explosions hurling all manner of debris high into the sky. Then a cloud of smoke began forming, to overhang a bowl-like depression in the earth still rumbling and belching flame.

The bungalows were gone, the big house was gone, the pier and its new building were gone—there was nothing down there but scorched earth and an artificial volcano.

Grimaldi whispered, "Man oh man. That's hard to believe."

Many things, Bolan could have told his friend of the Terrifying Flying Service, could be hard to believe.

But not that.

It was the hardest touch of Bolan's war against the mob. He believed it. A lot of discarnate souls were right now believing it. Damn right. And those that were left would believe it—and might think two times around before trying it again.

"Take me home, Jack," the Executioner said tiredly.

There was, thank God, still a home to return to.

EPILOG

Leo Turrin was standing outside the warwagon, awaiting the return of the warrior. He turned away, keeping his face down, until the chopper lifted away, then he came forward to hug the man about the waist and speak gruff words about heroic deeds.

"Go home, Leo," Bolan told him, grinning.

"Fast as a four engine jet can take me," the double-lifer replied. "Hal is welcome to what's left around here. You go, too, Sarge. Quick and far."

Bolan said, "Sure," still grinning.

"Well. Jocko's waiting patiently just down the road. Better go before he gets nervous and comes looking."

"Don't blow it now, guy. Good times are just around the corner."

Leo Turrin turned his back to that and went away, laughing like a crazy man.

Bolan stepped into his infernal machine and lit a cigarette, cranked the engine, and set his sights for somewhere "quick and far."

Nice town, Seattle. Nice people, too. Even the too young and too natural, especially artfully mature and ethically balanced.

But this warwagon was "home" for the warrior. Wherever she traveled, he would find war and nice people.

183

Quick and far.

That would be the next battle line. Always too quick and never quite far enough.

But that was Bolan's world, and he was stuck with it.

Worse still, perhaps, *it* was stuck with *him*.